A Waif of the Plains

Bret Harte

Contents

A WAIF OF THE PLAINS

BY

Bret Harte

A WAIF OF THE PLAINS.
CHAPTER I.

A LONG level of dull gray that further away became a faint blue, with, here and there darker patches that looked like water. At times an open space, blackened and burnt in an irregular circle, with a shred of newspaper, an old rag, or broken tin can lying in the ashes. Beyond these always a low dark line that seemed to sink into the ground at night, and rose again in the morning with the first light, but never otherwise changed its height and distance. A sense of always moving with some indefinite purpose, but of always returning at night to me same place—with the same surroundings, the same people, the same bedclothes, and the same awful black canopy dropped down from above. A chalky taste of dust on the mouth and lips, a gritty sense of earth, on the fingers, and an all-pervading heat and smell of cattle.

This was "The Great Plains" as they seemed to two children from the hooded depth of an emigrant wagon, above the swaying heads of toiling oxen, in the summer of 1852.

It had appeared so to them for two weeks, always the same and always without the least sense to them of wonder or monotony. When they viewed it from the road, walking beside the wagon, there was only the team itself added to the unvarying picture. One of the wagons bore on its canvas hood the inscription, in large black letters, "Off to California!" on the other "Root, Hog, or Die," but neither of them awoke in the minds of the children the faintest idea of playfulness or jocularity. Perhaps it was difficult to connect the serious men, who occasionally walked beside them and seemed to grow more taciturn and depressed as the day wore on, with this past effusive pleasantry.

Yet the impressions of the two children differed slightly. The eldest, a boy of eleven, was apparently new to the domestic habits and customs of a life to which the younger, a girl of seven, was evidently native and familiar. The food was coarse and less skillfully prepared than that to which he had been accustomed. There was a certain freedom and roughness in their intercourse, a simplicity that bordered almost on rudeness in their domestic arrangements, and a speech that was at times almost untranslatable to him. He slept in his clothes, wrapped up in blankets; he was conscious that in the matter of cleanliness he was left to himself to overcome the difficulties of finding water and towels. But it is doubtful if in his youthfulness it affected him more than a novelty. He ate and slept well, and found his life amusing. Only at times the rudeness of his companions, or, worse, an indifference that made him feel his dependency upon them, awoke a vague sense of some wrong that had been done to him which, while it was voiceless to all others and even uneasily put aside by himself, was still always slumbering in his childish consciousness.

To the party he was known as an orphan put on the train at "St. Jo" by some relative of his stepmother, to be delivered to another relative at Sacramento. As his stepmother had not even taken leave of him, but had entrusted his departure to the relative with whom he had been lately living, it was considered as an act of "riddance," and accepted as such by her party, and even vaguely acquiesced in by the boy himself. What consideration had been offered for his passage he did not know; he only remembered that he had been told "to make himself handy." This he had done cheerfully, if at times with the unskillfulness of a novice; but it was not a peculiar or a menial task in a company where all took part in manual labor, and where existence seemed to him to bear the charm of a prolonged picnic. Neither was he subjected to any difference of affection or treatment from Mrs. Silsbee, the mother of his little companion, and the wife of the leader of the train. Prematurely old, of ill-health, and harassed with cares, she had no time to waste in discriminating maternal tenderness for her daughter, but treated the children with, equal and unbiased querulousness.

The rear wagon creaked, swayed, and rolled on slowly and heavily. The hoofs of the draft-oxen, occasionally striking in me dust with a dull report, sent little pulls like smoke on either side of the track. Within, the children were playing "keeping store." The little girl, as an opulent and extravagant; customer, was purchasing of the boy, who sat behind a counter improvised from a nail-keg and the front seat, most of the available contents of the wagon, either under their own names or an imaginary one as the moment suggested, and paying for them in the easy and liberal currency of dried beans and bits of paper. Change was given by the expeditious method of tearing the paper into smaller fragments. The diminution of stock was remedied by buying the same article over again under a different name. Nevertheless, in spite of these favorable commercial conditions, the market seemed dull.

"I can show you a fine quality of sheeting at four cents a yard, double width," said the boy, rising and leaning on his fingers on the counter as he had seen the shopmen do. "All wool and will wash," he added, with easy gravity.

"I can buy it cheaper at Jackson's," said the girl, with the intuitive duplicity of her bargaining sex.

"Very well," said the boy. "I won't play any more."

"Who cares?" said the girl indifferently.

The boy here promptly upset the counter;' the rolled-up blanket which had deceitfully represented the desirable sheeting falling on the wagon floor. It apparently suggested a new idea to the former salesman. "I say! let's play 'damaged stock,' See, I'll tumble all the things down here right on top o' the others, and sell 'em for less than cost."

The girl looked up. The suggestion was bold, bad, and momentarily attractive. But I she only said "No," apparently from habit, picked up her doll, and the boy clambered to the front of the wagon. The incomplete episode terminated at once with that perfect forgetfulness, indifference, and irresponsibility common to all young animals. If either could have flown away or bounded off finally at that moment, they would have done so with no more concern for preliminary detail than a bird or squirrel. The wagon rolled steadily on. The boy could see that one of their teamsters had climbed up on the tail-board of the preceding vehicle. The other seemed to be walking in a dusty sleep.

"Kla'uns," said the girl.

The boy, without turning his head, responded, "Susy."

"Wot are you going to be? said the girl.

"Goin' to be?" repeated Clarence.

"When you is growed," explained Susy.

Clarence hesitated. His settled determination had been to become a pirate, merciless yet discriminating. But reading in a bethumbed "Guide to the Plains" that morning of Fort Laramie and Kit Carson, he had decided upon the career of a "scout," as being more accessible and requiring less water. Yet, out of compassion for Susy's possible ignorance, he said neither, and responded with the American boy's modest conventionality, "President." It was safe, required no embarrassing description, and had been approved by benevolent old gentlemen with, their hands on his head.

"I'm goin' to be a parson's wife," said Susy, "and keep hens, and have things giv' to me. Baby clothes, and apples, and apple sass—and melasses! and more baby clothes! and pork when you kill."

She had thrown herself at the bottom of the wagon, with her back towards him and her doll in her lap. He could see the curve of her curly head, and beyond, her bare dimpled knees, which were raised, and over which she was trying to fold the hem of her brief skirt.

"I wouldn't be a President's wife, she said presently.

"You couldn't!"

"Could if I wanted to!"

"Couldn't!"

"Could now!"

"Couldn't!"

"Why?"

Finding it difficult to explain his convictions of her ineligibility, Clarence thought it equally crushing not to give any. There was a long silence. It was very hot and dusty. The wagon scarcely seemed to move. Clarence gazed at the vignette of the track behind them formed by the hood of the rear. Presently he rose and walked past her to the tail-board. "Goin' to get down," he said, putting his legs over.

"Maw says 'No,'" said Susy.

Clarence did not reply, but dropped to the ground beside the slowly turning wheels. Without quickening his pace he could easily keep his hand on the tail-board.

"Kla'uns."

He looked up.

"Take me."

She had already clapped on her sun-bonnet and was standing at the edge of the tailboard, her little arms extended in such perfect confidence of being caught that the boy could not resist. He caught her cleverly. They halted a moment and let the lumbering vehicle move away from them, as it swayed from side to side as if laboring in a heavy sea. They remained motionless until it had reached nearly a hundred yards, and then, with a sudden half-real, half-assumed, but altogether delightful trepidation, ran forward and caught up with it again. This they repeated two or three times until both themselves and the excitement were exhausted, and they again plodded on hand in hand. Presently Clarence uttered a cry.

"My! Susy—look there!"

The rear wagon had once more slipped away from them a considerable distance. Between it and them, crossing its track, a most extraordinary creature had halted.

At first glance it seemed a dog—a discomfited, shameless, ownerless outcast of streets and byways, rather than an honest stray of some drover's train. It was so gaunt, so dusty, so greasy, so slouching, and so lazy! But as they looked at it more intently they saw that the grayish hair of its back had a bristly ridge, and there were great poisonous-looking dark blotches on its flanks, and that the slouch of its haunches was a peculiarity of its figure, and not the cowering of fear. As it lifted, its suspicious head towards them they could see that its thin lips, too short to cover its white teeth, were curled in a perpetual sneer.

"Here, doggie!" said Clarence excitedly. "Good dog! Come."

Susy burst into a triumphant laugh. "Ettain't no dog, silly; it's er coyote."

Clarence blushed. It wasn't the first time the pioneer's daughter had shown her superior knowledge. He said quickly, to hide his discomfiture, "I'll. ketch him, any way; he's nothin' mor'n a ki yi."

"Ye can't tho," said Susy, shaking her sun-bonnet. "He's faster nor a hoss!"

Nevertheless, Clarence ran towards him, followed by Susy. When they had come within twenty feet of him, the lazy creature, without apparently the least effort, took two or three limping bounds to one side, and remained at the same distance as before. They repeated, this onset three or four times with more or less excitement and hilarity, the animal evading them to one side, but never actually retreating before them. Finally, it occurred to them both that although they were not catching him they were not driving him away. The consequences of that thought were put into shape by Susy with round-eyed significance.

"Kla'uns, he bites."

Clarence picked up a hard sun-baked clod, and, running forward, threw it at the coyote. It was a clever shot, and struck him on his slouching haunches. He snapped, and gave a short snarling yelp, and vanished. Clarence returned with a victorious air to his companion. But she was gazing intently in the opposite direction, and for the first time he discovered that the coyote had been leading them half round a circle.

"Kla'uns," says Susy, with a hysterical little laugh.

"Well?"

"The wagon's gone."

Clarence started. It was true. Not only their wagon, but the whole train of oxen and teamsters had utterly disappeared, vanishing as completely as if they had been caught up in a whirlwind or engulfed in the earth! Even the low cloud of dust that usually marked their distant course by day was nowhere to be seen. The long level plain stretched before them to the setting sun, without a sign or trace of moving life or animation. That great blue crystal bowl, ruled with dust and fire by day, with stars and darkness by night, which had always seemed to drop its rim round them everywhere and shut them in, seemed to them now to have been lifted to let the train pass out, and then closed down upon them forever.

CHAPTER II

THEIR first sensation was one of purely animal freedom.

They looked at each other with sparkling eyes and long silent breaths. But this spontaneous outburst of savage nature soon passed. Susy's little hand presently reached forward and clutched Clarence's jacket. The boy understood it, and said quickly,—

"They ain't gone far, and they'll stop as soon as they find us gone."

They trotted on a little faster; the sun they had followed every day and the fresh wagon tracks being their unfailing guides; the keen, cool air of the plains, taking the place of that all-pervading dust and smell of the perspiring oxen, invigorating them with its breath.

"We ain't skeered a bit, are we? said Susy.

"What's there to be afraid of?" said Clarence scornfully. He said this none the less strongly because he suddenly remembered that they had been often left alone in the wagon for hours without being looked after, and that their absence might not be noticed until the train stopped to encamp at dusk, two hours later. They were not running very fast, yet either they were more tired than they knew, or the air was thinner, for they both seemed to breathe quickly. Suddenly Clarence stopped.

"There they are now."

He was pointing to a light cloud of dust in the far-off horizon, from which the black hulk of a wagon emerged for a moment and was lost. But even as they gazed the cloud seemed to sink like a fairy mirage to the earth again, the whole train disappeared, and only the empty stretching track returned. They did not know that this seemingly flat and level plain was really undulatory, and that the vanished train had simply dipped below their view on some further slope even as it had once before. But they knew they were disappointed, and that disappointment revealed to them the fact that they had concealed it from each other. The girl was the first to succumb, and burst into a quick spasm of angry tears. That single act of weakness called out the boy's pride and strength. There was no longer an equality of suffering; he had become her protector; he felt himself responsible for both. Considering her no longer his equal, he was no longer frank with her.

"There's nothin' to boo-hoo for," he said., with a half-affected brusqueness. "So quit, now! They'll stop in a minit, and send some one back for us. Shouldn't wonder if they're doin' it now."

But Susy, with feminine discrimination detecting the hollow ring in his voice, here threw herself upon him and began to beat him violently with her little fists. "They ain't! They ain't They ain't! You know it! How dare you?" Then, exhausted with her struggles, she suddenly threw herself flat on the dry grass, shut her eyes tightly, and clutched at the stubble.

"Get up," said the boy, with a pale, determined face that seemed to have got much older.

"You leave me be," said Susy.

"Do you want me to go away and leave you? "asked the boy.

Susy opened one blue eye furtively in the secure depths of her sun-bonnet, and gazed at his changed face.

"Ye-e-s."

He pretended to turn away, but really to look at the height of the sinking sun.

"Kla'uns!"

"Well?"

"Take me."

She was holding up her hands. He lifted her gently in his arms, dropping her head over his shoulder. "Now," he said cheerfully, "you keep a good lookout that way, and I this, I and we'll soon be there."

The idea seemed to please her. After Clarence had stumbled on for a few moments, she said, "Do you see anything, Kla'uns?"

"Not yet."

"No more don't I." This equality of perception apparently satisfied her. Presently she lay more limp in his arms. She was asleep.

The sun was sinking lower; it had already touched the edge of the horizon, and was level with his dazzled and straining eyes. At times it seemed to impede his eager search and task his vision. Haze and black spots floated across the horizon, and round wafers, like duplicates of the sun, glittered back from the dull surface of the plains. Then he resolved to look no more until he had counted fifty, a hundred, but always with the same result, the return of the empty, unending plains—the disk growing redder as it neared the horizon, the fire it seemed to kindle as it sank, but nothing more!

Staggering under his burden, he tried to distract himself by fancying how the discovery of their absence would be made. He heard the listless, half-querulous discussion about the locality that regularly pervaded the nightly camp. He heard the discontented voice of Jake Silsbee as he halted beside their wagon, and said, "Come out o' that now, you two, and mighty quick about it." He heard the command harshly repeated. He saw the look of irritation on Silsbee's dusty, bearded face, that followed his hurried glance into the empty wagon. He heard the query, "What's gone o' them limbs now?" handed from wagon to wagon. He heard a few oaths; Mrs. Silsbee's high rasping voice, abuse of himself, the hurried and discon-

tented detachment of a search party, Silsbee and one of the hired men, and vocif-
eration and blame. Blame always for himself, the elder, who might have "known
better!" A little fear, perhaps, but he could not fancy either pity or commiseration.
Perhaps the thought upheld his pride; under the prospect of sympathy he might
have broken down.

At last he stumbled, and stopped to keep himself from falling forward on his
face. He could go no further; his breath was spent; he was dripping with perspira-
tion; his legs were trembling under him; there was a roaring in his ears; round red
disks of the sun were scattered everywhere around him like spots of blood. To the
right of the trail there seemed to be a slight mound, where he could rest awhile,
and yet keep his watchful survey of the horizon. But on reaching it he found that
it was only a tangle of taller mesquite grass, into which he sank with his burden.
Nevertheless, if useless as a point of vantage, it afforded a soft couch for Susy, who,
seemed to have fallen quite naturally into her usual afternoon siesta, and in a mea-
sure it shielded her from a cold breeze that had sprung up from the west. Utterly
exhausted himself, but not daring to yield to the torpor that seemed to be creeping
over him, Clarence half sat, half knelt down beside her, supporting himself with
one hand, and, partly hidden in the long grass, kept his straining eyes fixed on the
lonely track.

The red disk was sinking lower. It seemed to have already crumbled away a
part of the distance with its eating fires. As it sank still lower, it shot out long, luminous rays, diverging fan-like across the plain, as if, in the boy's excited fancy, it too
were searching for the lost estrays. And as one long beam seemed to linger over his
hiding-place, he even thought that it might serve as a guide to Silsbee and the other
seekers, and was constrained to stagger to his feet, erect in its light. But it soon sank,
and with it Clarence dropped back again to his crouching watch. Yet he knew that
the daylight was still good for an hour, and with the withdrawal of that mystic sunset glory objects became even more distinct and sharply defined than at any other
time. And with the merciful sheathing of that flaming sword which seemed to have
waved between him and the vanished train, his eyes already felt a blessed relief.

CHAPTER III.

WITH the setting of the sun an ominous silence fell. He could, hear the low breathing of Susy, and even fancied he could hear the beating of his own heart in that oppressive hush of all nature. For the day's march had always been accompanied by the monotonous creaking of wheels and axles, and even the quiet of the night encampment had been always more or less broken by the movement of unquiet sleepers on the wagon beds, or the breathing of the cattle. But here there was neither sound nor motion. Susy's prattle, and even the sound of his own voice, would have broken the benumbing spell, but it was part of his growing self-denial now that he refrained from waking her even by a whisper. She would awaken soon enough to thirst and hunger, perhaps, and then what was he to do? If that looked-for help would only come now—while she still slept. For it was part of his boyish fancy that if he could, deliver her asleep, and undemonstrative of fear and suffering, he would be less blameful, and she less mindful of her trouble. If it did not come— but he would not think, of that yet! If she was thirsty meantime—well, it might rain, and there was always the dew which they used to brush oil the morning grass; he would take off his shirt and catch it in that, like a shipwrecked mariner. It would be funny, and make her laugh. For himself he would not laugh; he felt he was getting very old and grown up in this loneliness.

It was getting darker—they should be looking into the wagons now. A new doubt began to assail him. Ought he not, now that he was rested, make the most of the remaining moments of daylight, and before the glow faded from the west, when he would no longer have any bearings to guide him? But there was always the risk of waking her!—to what? The fear of being confronted again with *her* fear, and of being unable to pacify her, at last decided him to remain. But he crept softly through the grass, and in the dust of the track traced the four points of the compass, as he would, still determine them by the sunset light, with a large printed W to indicate the west! This boyish contrivance particularly pleased him. If he had only had a pole, a stick, or even a twig, on which to tie his handkerchief and erect it above the clump of mesquite as a signal to the searchers in case he should be overcome by fatigue or sleep, he would have been happy. But the plain was barren of brush or timber; he did not dream that this omission and the very unobtrusiveness of his hiding-place would be his salvation from a great danger.

With the coming darkness the wind arose and swept the plain with a long-drawn sigh. This increased to a murmur, till presently the whole expanse—before sunk in awful silence—seemed to awake with vague complaints, incessant sounds, and low meanings. At times he thought he heard the halloaing of distant voices, at times it seemed as a whisper in his own ear. In the silence that followed each blast he fancied he could detect the creaking of the wagon, the dull thud of the oxen's hoofs, or broken fragments of speech, blown and scattered even as he strained his ears to listen by the next gust. This tension of the ear began to confuse his brain, as his eyes had been previously dazzled by the sunlight, and a strange torpor began to steal over his faculties. Once or twice his head dropped.

He awoke with a start. A moving figure had suddenly uplifted itself between him and the horizon! It was not twenty yards away, so clearly outlined against the still luminous sky that it seemed even nearer. A human figure, but so disheveled, so fantastic, and yet so mean and puerile in its extravagance that it seemed the outcome of a childish dream. It was a mounted figure, but so ludicrously dispropor-tionate to the pony it bestrode, whose slim legs were stiffly buried in the dust in a breathless halt, that it might have been a straggler from some vulgar wandering circus. A tall hat, crown-less and brimless a castaway of civilization, surmounted by a turkey's feather, was on its head; over its shoulders hung a dirty tattered blanket that scarcely covered the two painted legs which seemed clothed in soiled yellow hose. In one hand it held a gun; the other was bent above its eyes in eager scrutiny of some distant point beyond and east of the spot where the children lay concealed. Presently, with a dozen quick noiseless strides of the pony's legs, the apparition moved to the right, its gaze still fixed on that mysterious part of the horizon. There was no mistaking it now! The painted Hebraic face, the large curved nose, the bony cheek, the broad mouth, the shadowed eyes, the straight long matted locks! It was an Indian! Not the picturesque creature of Clarence's imagination, but still an In-dian! The boy was uneasy, suspicious, antagonistic, but not afraid. He looked at the heavy animal face with the superiority of intelligence, at the half-naked figure with the conscious supremacy of dress, at the lower individuality with the contempt of a higher race. Yet a moment after, when the figure wheeled and disappeared towards the undulating west, a strange chill crept over him. Yet he did not know that in this puerile phantom and painted pigmy the awful majesty of Death had passed him by.

"Mamma!"

It was Susy's voice, struggling into consciousness. Perhaps she had been instinctively conscious of the boy's sudden fears.

"Hush!"

He had just turned to the objective point of the Indian's gaze. There *was* something! A dark line was moving along with the gathering darkness. For a moment he hardly dared to voice his thoughts even to himself. It was a following train overtaking them from the rear! And from the rapidity of its movements a train with horses, hurrying forward to evening camp. He had never dreamt of help from that quarter. This was what the Indian's keen eyes had been watching, and why he had so precipitately fled.

The strange train was now coming up at a round trot. It was evidently well appointed, with five or six large wagons and several outriders. In half an hour it would be here. Yet he refrained from waking Susy, who had fallen asleep again; his old superstition of securing her safety first being still uppermost. He took off his jacket to cover her shoulders, and rearranged her nest. Then he glanced again at the coming train. But for some unaccountable reason it had changed its direction, and instead of following the track that should have brought it to his side it had turned off to the left! In ten minutes it would pass abreast of him a mile and a half away! If he woke Susy now, he knew she would be helpless in her terror, and he could not carry her half that distance. He might rush to the train himself and return with help, but he would never leave her alone—in the darkness. Never! If she woke she would die of fright, perhaps, or wander blindly and aimlessly away. No! The train would pass, and with it that hope of rescue. Something was in his throat, but he gulped it down and was quiet again, albeit he shivered in the night wind.

The train was nearly abreast of him now. He ran out of the tall grass, waving his straw hat above his head in the faint hope of attracting attention. But he did not go far, for he found to his alarm that when he turned back again the clump of mesquite was scarcely distinguishable from the rest of the plain. This settled all question of his going. Even if he reached the train and returned with some one, how would he ever find her again in this desolate expanse?

He watched the train slowly pass—still mechanically, almost hopelessly, waving his hat as he ran up and down before the mesquite, as if he were waving a last farewell to his departing hope. Suddenly it appeared to him that three of the outriders who were preceding the first wagon had changed, their shape. They were no longer sharp, oblong, black blocks against the horizon, but had become at first blurred and indistinct, then taller and narrower, until at last they stood out like exclamation points against the sky. He continued to wave his hat, they continued to grow taller and narrower. He understood it now—the three transformed blocks were the outriders coming towards him.

This is what he had seen—

This is what he saw now—!!!

He ran back to Susy to see if she still slept, for his foolish desire to have her saved unconsciously was stronger than ever now that safety seemed so near. She was still sleeping, although she had moved slightly. He ran to the front again.

The outriders had apparently halted. What were they doing? Why wouldn't they come on?

Suddenly a blinding flash of light seemed to burst from one of them. Away over his head something whistled like a rushing bird, and sped oil invisible. They had fired a gun; they were signaling to him—Clarence—like a grown-up man. He would have given his life at that moment to have had a gun. But he could only wave his hat frantically.

One of the figures here bore away and impetuously darted forward again. He was coming nearer, powerful, gigantic, formidable, as he loomed through the darkness. All at once he threw up his arm with a wild gesture to the others; and his voice, manly, frank, and assuring, came ringing before him.

"Hold up! Good God! It's no Injin—it's a child!"

In another moment he had reined up beside Clarence and leaned, over nun, bearded, handsome, powerful, and protecting.

"Hallo! What's all this? What are you doing here?"

"Lost from Mr. Silsbee's train," said Clarence, pointing to the darkened west.

"Lost?—how long?"

"About three hours. I thought they'd come back for us," said Clarence apologetically to this big, kindly man.

And you kalkilated to wait here for 'em?"

"Yes, yes—I did—till I saw you."

"Then why m thunder didn't you light out straight for us, instead of hanging round here and drawing us out?"

The boy hung his head. He knew his reasons were unchanged, but all at once they seemed very foolish and unmanly to speak out.

"Only that we were on the keen jump for Injins," continued the stranger, "we wouldn't have seen you at all, and might hev shot you when we did. What possessed you to stay here?"

The boy was still silent. "Kla'uns," said a faint, sleepy voice from the mesquite, "take me." The rifle-shot had awakened Susy.

The stranger turned quickly towards the sound. Clarence started and recalled, himself. "There," he said bitterly, "you've done it now, you've wakened her! ***That's*** why I stayed. I couldn't carry her over there to you. I couldn't let her walk, for she'd be frightened. I wouldn't wake her up, for she'd be frightened, and I mightn't find her again. There!" He had made up his mind to be abused, but he was reckless now that she was safe.

The men glanced at each other. "Then," said the spokesman quietly, "you didn't strike out for us on account of your sister?

"She ain't my sister," said Clarence quickly. "She's a little girl. She's Mrs. Silsbee's little girl. We were in the wagon and got down. It's my fault. I helped her down."

The three men reined their horses closely round him, leaning forward from their saddles, with their hands on their knees and their heads on one side. Then, said the spokesman gravely, you just reckoned to stay here, old man, and take your chances with her rather than run the risk of frightening or leaving her—though it was your one chance of life!"

"Yes," said the boy, scornful of this feeble, grown-up repetition.

"Come here."

The boy came doggedly forward. The man pushed back the well-worn straw hat from Clarence's forehead and looked into his lowering face. With his hand still on the boy's head he turned him round to the others, and said quietly,—

"Suthin of a pup, eh?"

"You bet," they responded.

The voice was not unkindly, although the speaker had thrown Ins lower jaw forward as to pronounce the word "pup" with a humorous suggestion of a mastiff. Before Clarence could make up his mind if the epithet was insulting or not, the man put out his stirruped foot, and, with a gesture of invitation, said, "Jump up."

"But Susy," said Clarence, drawing back.

"Look; she's making up to Phil already."

Clarence looked. Susy had crawled out of the mesquite, and with her sun-bonnet hanging down her back, her curls tossed around her face, still flushed with sleep, and Clarence's jacket over her shoulders, was gazing up with grave satisfaction in the laughing eyes of one of the men who was with outstretched hands bending over her. Could he believe his senses? The terror-stricken, willful, unmanageable Susy, whom he would have translated unconsciously to safety without this terrible ordeal of being awakened to the loss of her home and parents at any sacrifice to himself—this ingenuous infant was absolutely throwing herself with every appearance of forgetfulness into the arms of the first new-comer! Yet his perception of this fact was accompanied by no sense of ingratitude. For her sake he felt relieved, and with a boyish smile of satisfaction and encouragement vaulted into the saddle before the stranger.

CHAPTER IV.

THE dash forward to the train, securely held in the saddle by the arms of their deliverers, was a secret joy to the children that seemed only too quickly over. The resistless gallop of the fiery mustangs, the rush of the night wind, the gathering darkness in which the distant wagons, now halted and facing them, looked like domed huts in the horizon—all these seemed but a delightful and fitting climax to the events or, the day. In the sublime forgetfulness of youth, all they had gone through had left no embarrassing record behind it; they were willing to repeat their experiences on the morrow, confident of some equally happy end. And when

Clarence, timidly reaching his hand towards the horse-hair reins lightly held by his companion, had them playfully yielded up to him by that bold and confident rider, the boy felt himself indeed a man.

But a greater surprise was in store for them. As they neared the wagons, now formed into a circle with a certain degree of military formality, they could see that the appointments of the strange party were larger and more liberal than their own, or indeed anything they had ever known of the kind. Forty or fifty horses were tethered within the circle, and the camp fires were already blazing. Before one of them a large tent was erected, and through the parted flaps could be seen a table actually spread with a white cloth. Was it a school feast, or was this their ordinary household arrangement? Clarence and Susy thought of their own dinners, usually laid on bare boards beneath the sky, or under the low hood of the wagon in rainy weather, and marveled. And when they finally halted, and were lifted from their horses, and passed one wagon fitted up as a bedroom and another as a kitchen, they could only nudge each other with silent appreciation. But here again the difference already noted in the equality of the sensations of the two children was observable. Both were equally and agreeably surprised. But Susy's wonder was merely the sense of novelty and inexperience, and a slight disbelief in the actual necessity of what she saw; while Clarence, whether from some previous general experience or peculiar temperament, had the conviction that what he saw here was the usual custom, and what he had known with the Silsbees was the novelty. The feeling was attended with a slight sense of wounded pride for Susy, as if her enthusiasm had exposed her to ridicule.

The man who had carried him, and seemed to be the head of the party, had already preceded them to the tent, and presently reappeared with a lady with whom he had exchanged a dozen hurried words. They seemed to refer to him and Susy; but Clarence was too much preoccupied with the fact that the lady was pretty, that her clothes were neat and thoroughly clean, that her hair was tidy and not rumpled, and that, although she wore an apron, it was as clean as her gown, and even had ribbons on it, to listen to what was said. And when she ran eagerly forward, and with a fascinating smile lifted the astonished Susy in her arms, Clarence, in his delight for his young charge, quite forgot that she had not noticed him. The bearded man, who seemed to be the lady's husband, evidently pointed out the omission, with some additions that Clarence could not catch; for after saying, with a pretty pout, "Well, why shouldn't he?" she came forward with the same dazzling smile, and laid her small and clean white hand, upon his shoulder.

"And so you took good care of the dear little thing? She's such an angel, isn't she? and you must love her very much."

Clarence colored with delight. It was true it had never occurred to him to look at Susy in the light of a celestial visitant, and I fear he was just then more struck with the fair complimenter than the compliment to his companion, but he was pleased for her sake. He was not yet old enough to be conscious of the sex's belief m its irresistible domination over mankind at all ages, and that Johnny in his check apron would be always a hopeless conquest of Jeannette in her pinafore, and that he ought to have been in love with Susy.

Howbeit, the lady suddenly whisked her away to the recesses of her own wagon, to reappear later, washed, curled, and be-rib-boned like a new doll, and Clarence was left alone with the husband and another of the party.

"Well, my boy, you haven't told me your name yet."

"Clarence, sir."

"So Susy calls you, but what else?"

"Clarence Brant."

"Any relation to Colonel Brant?" asked the second man carelessly.

"He was my father," said the boy, brightening under this faint prospect of recognition in his loneliness.

The two men glanced at each other. The leader looked at the boy curiously, and said,—

"Are you the son of Colonel Brant, of Louisville?"

"Yes, sir," said, the boy, with a dim stirring of uneasiness in his heart. "But he's dead now," he added finally.

"Ah, when did he die?" said the man quickly.

"Oh, a long time ago. I don't remember him much. I was very little," said the boy, half apologetically.

"Ah, you don't remember him?"

"No," said Clarence shortly. He was beginning to fall back upon that certain dogged repetition which in sensitive children arises from their hopeless inability to express their deeper feelings. He also had an instinctive consciousness that this want of a knowledge of his father was part of that vague wrong that had been done him. It did not help his uneasiness that he could see that one of the two men, who turned away with a half-laugh, misunderstood or did not believe him.

"How did you come with the Silsbees?" asked the first man.

Clarence repeated mechanically, with a child's distaste of practical details, how he had lived with an aunt at St. Jo, and how his stepmother had procured his passage with the Silsbees to California, where he was to meet his cousin. All this with a lack of interest and abstraction that he was miserably conscious told against him, but he was yet helpless to resist.

The first man remained thoughtful, and then glanced at Clarence's sunburnt hands. Presently his large, good-humored smile re-turned.

"Well, I suppose you are hungry?"

"Yes," said Clarence shyly. "But"—

"But what?"

"I should, like to wash myself a little," he returned hesitatingly, thinking of the clean tent, the clean lady, and Susy's ribbons.

"Certainly," said his friend, with a pleased look. "Come with me." Instead of leading Clarence to the battered tin basin and bar of yellow soap which had formed the toilet service or the Silsbee party, he brought the boy into one of the wagons, where there was a washstand, a china basin, and a cake of scented soap. Standing beside Clarence, he watched him perform his ablutions with an approving air which rather embarrassed his protégé. Presently he said, almost abruptly,—

"Do you remember your father's house at Louisville?"

"Yes, sir; but it was a long time ago." Clarence remembered it as being very different from his home at St. Joseph's, but from some innate feeling of diffidence he would have shrunk from describing it in that way. He, however, said he thought it was a large house. Yet the modest answer only made his new friend look at him the more keenly.

"Your father was Colonel Hamilton Brant, of Louisville, wasn't he?" he said, half confidentially.

"Yes," said Clarence hopelessly.

"Well," said his friend cheerfully, as if dismissing an abstruse problem from his mind, let's go to supper."

When they reached the tent again, Clarence noticed that the supper was laid only for his host and wife and the second man,—who was familiarly called "Harry," but who spoke of the former always as "Mr. and Mrs. Peyton,"—while the remainder of the party, a dozen men, were at a second camp fire, and evidently enjoying themselves in a picturesque fashion. Had the boy been allowed to choose, he would have joined them, partly because it seemed more "manly," and partly that he dreaded a renewal of the questions.

But here, Susy, sitting bolt upright on an extemporized high stool, happily diverted his attention by pointing to the empty chair beside her.

"Kla'uns," she said suddenly, with her usual clear and appalling frankness, "they is chickens, and hamanaigs, and hot biksquits, and lasses, and Mister Peyton says I kin have 'em all."

Clarence, who had begun suddenly to feel that he was responsible for Susy's deportment, and was balefully conscious that she was holding her plated fork in her chubby fist by its middle, and, from his previous knowledge of her, was likely at any moment to plunge it into the dish before her, said softly,—

"Hush!"

"Yes, you shall, dear," said Mrs. Peyton, with tenderly beaming assurance to Susy and a half-reproachful glance at the boy. "Eat what you like, darling."

"It's a fork," whispered the still uneasy Clarence, as Susy now seemed inclined to stir her bowl of milk with it.

" 'T ain't, now, Kla'uns, it's only a split spoon," said Susy.

But Mrs. Peyton, in her rapt admiration, took small note of these irregularities, plying the child with food, forgetting her own meal, and only stopping at times to hit back the forward straying curls on Susy's shoulders. Mr. Peyton looked on gravely and contentedly. Suddenly the eyes of husband and wife met.

"She'd have been nearly as old as this, John, said Mrs. Peyton, in a faint voice.

John Peyton nodded without speaking, and turned his eyes away into the gathering darkness. The man "Harry" also looked abstractedly at his plate, as if he was saying grace. Clarence wondered who "she" was, and why two little tears dropped from Mrs. Peyton's lashes into Susy's milk, and whether Susy might not violently object to it. He did not know until later that the Peytons had lost their only child, and Susy comfortably drained this mingled cup of a mother's grief and tenderness without suspicion.

"I suppose we'll come up with their train early to-morrow, if some of them don't find us to-night," said Mrs. Peyton, with a long sigh and a regretful glance at Susy. "Perhaps we might travel together for a little while," she added timidly.

Harry laughed, and Mr. Peyton replied gravely, "I am afraid we wouldn't travel with them, even for company's sake; and," he added, in a lower and graver voice, "it's rather odd the search, party hasn't come upon us yet, though I'm keeping Pete and Hank patrolling the trail to meet them."

"It's heartless—so it is!" said Mrs. Peyton, with sudden indignation. "It would be all very well if it was only this boy, who an take care of himself; but to be so careless of a mere baby like this, it's shameful!"

For the first time, Clarence tasted, the cruelty of discrimination. All the more keenly that he was beginning to worship, after his boyish fashion, this sweet-faced, clean, and tender-hearted woman. Perhaps Mr. Peyton noticed it, for he came quietly to his aid.

"May be they know better than we in what careful hands they had left her," he said, with a cheerful nod towards Clarence. "And, again, they may have been fooled as we were by Injin signs and left the straight road.

This suggestion instantly recalled to Clarence his vision in the mesquite. Should he dare tell them? Would they believe him, or would they laugh at him before her? He hesitated, and at last resolved to tell it privately to the husband. When the meal was ended, and he was made happy by Mrs. Peyton's laughing acceptance of his offer to help her clear the table and wash the dishes, they all gathered comfortably in front of the tent before the large camp fire. At the other fire the rest of the party were playing cards and laughing, but Clarence no longer cared to join them. He was quite tranquil in the maternal propinquity of his hostess, albeit a little uneasy as to his reticence about the Indian.

"Kla'uns," said Susy, relieving a momentary pause, in her highest voice, "knows how to speak. Speak, Kla'uns!"

It appearing from Clarence's blushing explanation that this gift was not the ordinary faculty of speech, but a capacity to recite verse, he was politely pressed by the company for a performance.

"Speak 'em, Kla'uns, the boy what stood unto the burnin' deck, and said, 'The boy, oh, where was he?' " said Susy, comfortably lying down on Mrs. Peyton's lap, and contemplating her bare knees in the air. "It's 'bout a boy," she added confidentially to Mrs. Peyton, "whose father wouldn't never, never stay with him on a burnin' ship, though he said, 'Stay, father, stay,' ever so much."

With this clear, lucid, and perfectly satisfactory explanation of Mrs. Hemans's "Casabianca," Clarence began. Unfortunately, his actual rendering of this popular school performance was more an effort of memory than anything else, and was illustrated by those wooden gestures which a Western schoolmaster had taught him. He described the names that "roared around him," by indicating with his hand a perfect circle, of which he was the axis; he adjured his father, the late Admiral Casabianca, by clasping his hands before his chin, as if wanting to be manacled in an attitude which he was miserably conscious was unlike anything he himself had ever felt or seen before; he described that father "faint in death below," and "the flag on high," with one single motion. Yet something that the verses had kindled in his active imagination, perhaps, rather than an illustration of the verses themselves, at times brightened his gray eyes, became tremulous in his youthful voice, and I fear occasionally incoherent on his lips. At times, when not conscious of his affected art, the plain and all upon it seemed to him to slip away into the night, the blazing camp fire at his feet to wrap him in a fateful glory, and a vague devotion to something—he knew not what—so possessed him that he communicated it, and probably some of his own youthful delight in extravagant voice, to his hearers, until, when he ceased with a glowing face, he was surprised to find that the card players had deserted their camp fires and gathered round the tent.

CHAPTER V.

"YOU didn't say 'Stay, father, stay,' enough, Kla'uns," said Susy critically. Then suddenly starting upright in Mrs. Peyton's lap, she continued rapidly, "I kin dance. And sing. I kin dance High Jambooree."

"What's High Jambooree, dear?" asked Mrs. Peyton.

"You'll see. Lemme down." And Susy slipped to the ground.

The dance of High Jambooree, evidently of remote mystical African origin, appeared to consist of three small skips to the right and then to the left, accompanied by the holding up of very short skirts, incessant "teetering" on the toes of small feet, the exhibition of much bare knee and stocking, and a gurgling accompaniment of childish laughter. Vehemently applauded, it left the little performer breathless, but invincible and ready for fresh conquest.

"I kin sing, too," she gasped hurriedly, as if unwilling that the applause should lapse. "I kin sing. Oh, dear! Kla'uns," piteously, "*what* is it I sing?"

"Ben Bolt," suggested Clarence.

"Oh, yes. Oh, don't you remember sweet Alers Ben Bolt?" began Susy, in the same breath and the wrong key. "Sweet Alers, with hair so brown, who wept with delight when you giv'd her a smile, and"—with knitted brows and appealing recitative, "what's er rest of it, Kla'uns?"

"Who trembled with fear at your frown?" prompted Clarence.

"Who trembled with fear at my frown?" shrilled Susy. "I forget er rest. Wait! I kin sing"—

"Praise God," suggested Clarence.

"Yes." Here Susy, a regular attendant in camp and prayer meetings, was on firmer ground.

Promptly lifting her high treble, yet with a certain acquired deliberation, she began, "Praise God, from whom all blessings flow." At the end of the second line the whispering and laughing ceased. A deep voice to the right, that of the champion poker player, suddenly rose on the swell of the third line. He was instantly followed by a dozen ringing voices, and by the time the last line was reached it was given with a full chorus, in which the dull chant of teamsters and drivers mingled with the soprano of Mrs. Peyton and Susy's childish treble. Again and again it was repeated, with forgetful eyes and abstracted faces, rising and falling with the night wind and the leap and gleam of the camp fires, and fading again like them in the immeasurable mystery of the darkened plain.

In the deep and embarrassing silence that followed, at last the party hesitatingly broke up, Mrs. Peyton retiring with Susy after offering the child to Clarence for a perfunctory "good-night" kiss, an unusual proceeding, which somewhat astonished them both—and Clarence found himself near Mr. Peyton.

"I think," said Clarence timidly, "I saw an Injin to-day."

Mr. Peyton bent down towards him. "An Injin—where?" he asked quickly, with the same look of doubting interrogatory with which he had received Clarence's name and parentage.

The boy for a moment regretted having spoken. But with his old doggedness he particularized his statement. Fortunately, being gifted with a keen perception, he was able to describe the stranger accurately, and to impart with his description that contempt for its subject which he had felt, and which to his frontier auditor established its truthfulness. Peyton turned abruptly away, but presently returned with Harry and another man.

"You are sure of this?" said Peyton, half encouragingly.

"Yes, sir."

"As sure as you are that your fattier is Colonel Brant and is dead?" said Harry, with a light laugh.

Tears sprang into the boy's lowering eyes. "I don't lie," he said doggedly.

"I believe you, Clarence," said Peyton quietly. "But why didn't you say it before?"

"I didn't like to say it before Susy and—her!" stammered the boy.

"Her?"

"Yes, sir,—Mrs. Peyton," said Clarence blushingly.

"Oh," said Harry sarcastically, "how blessed polite we are!"

"That'll do. Let up on him, will you?" said Peyton, roughly, to his subordinate. "The boy knows what he's about. But," he continued, addressing Clarence, "how was it the Injin didn't see you?"

"I was very still on account of not waking Susy," said Clarence, "and"—He hesitated.

"And what?"

"He seemed more keen watching what *you* were doing," said the boy boldly.

"That's so," broke in the second man, who happened to be experienced, "and as he was to wind'ard o' the boy he was off *his* scent and bearings. He was one of their rear scouts; the rest o' them 's ahead crossing our track to cut us off. Ye didn't see anything else?"

"I saw a coyote first," said Clarence, greatly encouraged.

"Hold on!" said the expert, as Harry turned away with a sneer. "That's a sign, too. Wolf don't go where wolf hez been, and coyote don't foller Injins—there's no pickin's! How long afore did you see the coyote?"

"Just after we left the wagon," said Clarence.

"That's it," said the man, thoughtfully. "He was driven on ahead, or hanging on their flanks. These Injins are betwixt us and that ar train, or following it."

Peyton made a hurried gesture of warning, as if reminding the speaker of Clarence's presence—a gesture which the boy noticed and wondered at. Then the conversation of the three men took a lower tone, although Clarence distinctly heard the concluding opinion of the expert.

"It ain't no good now, Mr. Peyton, and you'd be only exposing yourself on their ground by breakin' camp agin to-night. And you don't know that it ain't *us* they're watchin'. You see, if we hadn't turned ore the straight road when we got that first scare from these yer lost children, we might hev gone on and walked plump into some cursed trap of those devils. To my mind, we're just in nigger luck, and with a good watch and my patrol we 're all right to be fixed where we be till daylight."

Mr. Peyton presently turned away, taking Clarence with him. "As we'll be up early and on the track of your tram to-morrow, my boy, you had better turn in now. I've put you up in my wagon, and as I expect to be in the saddle most of the night, I reckon I won't trouble you much." He led the way to a second wagon—drawn up beside the one where Susy and Mrs. Peyton had retired—which Clarence was surprised to find fitted with a writing table and desk, a chair, and even a bookshelf containing some volumes. A long locker, fitted like a lounge, had been made up as a couch for him, with the unwonted luxury of clean white sheets and pillow-cases. A soft matting covered the floor of the heavy wagon bed, which, Mr. Peyton explained, was hung on centre springs to prevent jarring. The sides and roof of the vehicle were of lightly paneled wood, instead of the usual hooked canvas frame of the ordinary emigrant wagon, and fitted with a glazed door and movable window for light and air. Clarence wondered why the big, powerful man, who seemed at home on horseback, should ever care to sit in this office like a merchant or a lawyer; and if this train sold things to the other trains, or took goods, like the peddlers, to towns on the route; but there seemed to be nothing to sell, and the other wagons were filled with only the goods required by the party. He would have liked to ask Mr. Peyton who *he* was, and have questioned *him* as freely as he himself had been questioned. But as the average adult man never takes into consideration the injustice of denying to the natural and even necessary curiosity of childhood that questioning which he himself is so apt to assume without right, and almost always without delicacy, Clarence had no recourse. Yet the boy, like all children, was conscious that if he had been afterwards questioned about *this* inexplicable experience, he would have been blamed for his ignorance concerning it. Left to himself presently, and ensconced between the sheets, he lay for some moments staring about him. The unwonted comfort of his couch, so different from the stuffy blanket in the hard wagon bed which he had shared with one of the teamsters, and the novelty, order, and cleanliness of his surroundings, while they were grateful to his instincts, began in some vague way to depress him. To his loyal nature it seemed a tacit infidelity to his former rough companions to be lying here; he had a dim idea that he had lost that independence which equal discomfort and equal pleasure among them had given him. There seemed a sense of servitude in accepting this luxury which was not his. This set him endeavoring to remember something of his father's house, of the large rooms, drafty staircases, and far-off ceilings, and the cold formality of a life that seemed made up of strange faces; some stranger—his parents; some kinder—the servants; particularly the black nurse who had him in charge. Why did Mr. Peyton ask him about it? Why, if it were so important to strangers, had not his mother told him more of it? And why was she not like this good woman with the gentle voice who was so kind, to—to Susy? And what did they mean by making *him* so miserable? Something rose m Jus throat, but with an effort he choked it back, and, creeping from the lounge, went softly to the window, opened it to see if it would work, and looked out. The shrouded camp fires, the stars that glittered but gave no light, the dim moving bulk of a patrol beyond the circle, all seemed to intensify the darkness, and changed the current of his thoughts. He remembered what Mr. Peyton had said of him, when they first met. "Suthin of a pup, ain't he?" Surely that meant something that was not bad! He crept back to the couch again.

Lying there, still awake, he reflected that he wouldn't be a scout when he grew up, but would be something like Mr. Peyton, and have a tram like this, and invite the Silsbees and Susy to accompany him. For this purpose, he and Susy, early tomorrow morning, would get permission to come in here and play at that game. This would familiarize him with the details, so that he would, be able at any time to take charge or it. He was already an authority on the subject of Indians! He had once been fired at—as an Indian. He would always carry a rifle like that hanging from the hooks at the end of the wagon before him, and would eventually slay many Indians and keep an account of them in a big book like that on the desk. Susy would help him, having grown up a lady, and they would both together issue provisions and rations from the door of the wagon to the gathered crowds. He would be known as the "White Chief," Ins Indian name being "Suthin of a Pup." He would have a circus van attached to the train, in which he would occasionally perform. He would also have artillery for protection. There would be a terrific engagement, and he would rush into the wagon, heated and blackened with gunpowder; and Susy would put down an account of it in a book, and Mrs. Peyton—for she would be there in some vague capacity—would say, "Really, now, I don't see but what we were very lucky in having such a boy as Clarence with us. I begin to understand him better." And Harry, who, for purposes of vague poetical retaliation, would also drop in at that moment, would mutter and say, "He is certainly the son of Colonel Brant; dear me!" and apologize. And his mother would come in also, in her coldest and most indifferent manner, in a white ball dress, and start and say, "Good gracious, how that boy has grown! I am sorry I did not see more of him when he was young." Yet even in the midst of this came a confusing numbness, and then the side of the wagon seemed to melt away, and he drifted out again alone into the empty desolate plain from which even the sleeping Susy had vanished, and he was left deserted and forgotten. Then all was quiet in the wagon, and only the night wind moving round it. But lo! the lashes of the sleeping White Chief—the dauntless leader, the ruthless destroyer of Indians—were wet with glittering tears!

Yet it seemed only a moment afterwards that he awoke with a faint consciousness of some arrested motion. To his utter consternation, the sun, three hours high, was shining in the wagon, already hot and stifling in its beams. There was the familiar smell and taste of the dirty road in the air about him. There was a faint creaking of boards and springs, a slight oscillation, and beyond the audible rattle of harness, as if the tram had been under way, the wagon moving, and then there had been a sudden halt. They had probably come up with the Silsbee train; in a few moments the change would be effected and all of his strange experience would be over. He must get up now. Yet, with the morning laziness of the healthy young animal, he curled up a moment longer in his luxurious couch.

How quiet it was! There were far-off voices, but they seemed suppressed and hurried. Through the window he saw one of the teamsters run rapidly past him with a strange, breathless, preoccupied face, halt a moment at one of the following wagons, and then run back again to the front. Then two of the voices came nearer, with the dull beating of hoofs in the dust.

"Rout out the boy and ask him, said a half-suppressed, impatient voice, which Clarence at once recognized as the man Harry's.

"Hold on till Peyton comes up," said the second voice, in a low tone; "leave it to him."

"Better find out what they were like, at once," grumbled Harry.

"Wait, stand back, said Peyton's voice, joining the others;" "*I'll* ask him."

Clarence looked wonderingly at the door. It opened on Mr. Peyton, dusty and dismounted, with a strange, abstracted look m his face.

"How many wagons are in your train, Clarence?"

"Three, sir."

"Any marks on them?"

"Yes, sir," said Clarence, eagerly: " 'Off to California' and 'Root, Hog, or Die.' "

Mr. Peyton's eye seemed to leap up and hold Clarence's with a sudden, strange significance, and then looked down.

"How many were you in all?" he continued.

"Five, and there was Mrs. Silsbee."

"No other woman?"

"No."

"Get up and dress yourself," he said gravely, and wait here till I come back. Keep cool and have your wits about you." He dropped his voice slightly. "Perhaps something's happened that you'll have to show yourself a little man again for, Clarence!"

The door closed, and the boy heard the same muffled hoofs and voices die away towards the front. He began to dress himself mechanically, almost vacantly, yet conscious always of a vague undercurrent of thrilling excitement. When he had finished he waited almost breathlessly, feeling the same beating of his heart that he had felt when he was following the vanished tram the day before. At last he could stand the suspense no longer, and opened the door. Everything was still in the motionless caravan, except—it struck him oddly even then—the unconcerned prattling voice of Susy from one of the nearer wagons. Perhaps a sudden feeling that this was something that concerned *her*, perhaps an irresistible impulse, overcame him, but the next moment he had leaped to the ground, faced about, and was running feverishly to the front.

The first thing that met his eyes was the helpless and desolate bulk of one of the Silsbee wagons a hundred rods away, bereft of oxen and pole, standing alone and motionless against the dazzling sky! Near it was the broken frame of another wagon, its fore wheels and axles gone, pitched forward on its knees like an ox under the butcher's sledge. Not far away there were the burnt and blackened ruins of a third, around which the whole party on foot and horseback seemed to be gathered. As the boy ran violently on, the group opened to make way for two men carrying some helpless but awful object between them. A terrible instinct made Clarence swerve from it in his headlong course, but he was at the same moment discovered by the others, and a cry arose of "Go back!" "Stop!" "Keep him back!" Heeding it no more than the wind, that whistled by him, Clarence made directly for the foremost wagon—the one in which he and Susy had played. A powerful hand caught his shoulder; it was Mr. Peyton's.

"Mrs. Silsbee's wagon," said the boy, with white lips, pointing to it. "Where is she?"

"She's missing," said Peyton, "and one other—the rest are dead."

"She must be there," said the boy, struggling, and pointing to the wagon; "let me go."

"Clarence," said Peyton sternly, accenting his grasp upon the boy's arm, "be a man! Look around you. Try and tell us who these are."

There seemed to be one or two heaps of old clothes lying on the ground, and further on, where the men at a command from Peyton had laid down their burden, another. In those ragged, dusty heaps of clothes, from which all the majesty of life seemed to have been ruthlessly stamped out, only what was ignoble and grotesque appeared to be left. There was nothing terrible in this. The boy moved slowly towards them; and, incredible even to himself, the overpowering fear of them that a moment before had overcome him left him as suddenly. He walked from the one to the other, recognizing them by certain marks and signs, and mentioning name after name. The groups gazed at him curiously; he was conscious that he scarcely understood himself, still less the same quiet purpose that now made him turn towards the furthest wagon.

"There's nothing there," said Peyton; "we've searched it." But the boy, without replying, continued his way, and the crowd followed him.

The deserted wagon, more rude, disorderly, and slovenly than it had ever seemed to him before, was now heaped and tumbled with broken bones, cans, scattered provisions, pots, pans, blankets, and clothing in the foul confusion of a dust-heap. But in this heterogeneous mingling the boy's quick eye caught sight of a draggled edge of calico.

"That's Mrs. Silsbee's dress!" he cried, and leapt into the wagon.

At first the men stared at each other, but an instant later a dozen hands were helping mm, nervously digging and clearing away the rubbish. Then one man uttered a sudden cry, and fell back with frantic but furious eyes uplifted against the pitiless, smiling sky above him.

"Great God! look here!"

It was the yellowish, waxen face of Mrs. Silsbee that had been uncovered. But to the fancy of the boy it had changed; the old familiar lines of worry, care, and querulous-ness had given way to a look of remote peace and statue-like repose. He had often vexed her in her aggressive life; he was touched with remorse at her cold, passionless apathy now, and pressed timidly forward. Even as he did so, the man, with a quick but warning gesture, hurriedly threw his handkerchief over the matted locks, as if to shut out something awful from his view. Clarence felt himself drawn back; but not before the white lips of a bystander had whispered a single word—

"Scalped, toot by God!"

CHAPTER VI.

Then followed days and weeks that seemed to Clarence as a dream. At first, an interval of hushed and awed restraint, when he and Susy were kept apart, a strange and artificial interest taken little note of by him, but afterwards remembered when others had forgotten it; the burial of Mrs. Silsbee beneath a cairn of stones, with some ceremonies that, simple though they were, seemed to usurp the sacred rights of grief from him and Susy, and leave them cold and frightened; days of frequent and incoherent childish outbursts from Susy, growing fainter and rarer as time went on, until they ceased, he knew not when; the haunting by night of that morning vision of the three or four heaps of ragged, clothes upon the ground, and a half regret that he had not examined them more closely; a recollection of the awful loneliness and desolation of the broken and abandoned wagon left behind on its knees, as if praying mutely when the train went on and left it; the trundling behind of the fateful wagon in which Mrs. Silsbee's body had been found, superstitiously shunned by every one, and when at last turned over to the authorities at an outpost garrison, seeming to drop the last link from the dragging chain of the past. The revelation to the children of a new experience in that brief glimpse of the frontier garrison; the handsome officer in uniform and belted sword, an heroic, vengeful figure to be admired and imitated hereafter; the sudden importance and respect given to Susy and himself as "survivors;" the sympathetic questioning and kindly exaggerations of their experiences, quickly accepted by Susy—all these, looking back upon them afterwards, seemed to have passed in a dream.

No less strange and visionary to them seemed the real transitions they noted, from the moving train. How one morning they missed the changeless, motionless, low, dark line along the horizon, and before noon found themselves among rocks and trees and a swiftly rushing river. How there suddenly appeared beside them a few days later a great gray cloud-covered ridge of mountains that they were convinced was that same dark line that they had seen so often. How the men laughed at them, and said that for the last three days they had been *crossing* that dark line, and that it was *higher* than the great gray-clouded range before them, which it had always hidden from their view! How Susy firmly believed that these changes took place in her sleep, when she always kinder felt they were crawlin' up," and how Clarence, in the happy depreciation of extreme youth, expressed his conviction that they "weren't a bit high, after all." How the weather became cold, though it was already summer, and at night the camp fire was a necessity, and there was a stove in the tent with Susy; and yet how all this faded away, and they were again upon a dazzling, burnt, and sun-dried plain! But always as in a dream!

More real were the persons who composed the party—whom they seemed to have always known—and who, in the innocent caprice of children, had become to them more actual than the dead had ever been. There was Mr. Peyton, who they now knew owned the train, and who was so rich that he "needn't go to California if he didn't want to, and was going to buy a great deal of it if he liked it," and who was also a lawyer and "policeman"—which was Susy's rendering of "politician"—and was called "Squire" and "Judge" at the frontier outpost, and could order anybody to be took up if he wanted to, and who knew everybody by their Christian names; and Mrs. Peyton, who had been delicate, and was ordered by the doctor to live in the open air for six months, and "never go into a house or a town agin," and who was going to adopt Susy as soon as her husband could arrange with Susy's relatives, and draw up the papers! How "Harry" was Henry Benham, Mrs. Peyton's brother, and a kind of partner of Mr. Peyton. And how the scout's name was Gus Gilder-sleeve, or the "White Crow," and how, through his recognized intrepidity, an attack upon their train was no doubt averted. Then there was "Bill," the stock herder, and "Texas Jim," the *vaquero*—the latter marvelous and unprecedented in horseman-ship. Such were their companions, as appeared through the gossip of the train and their own inexperienced consciousness. To them, they were all astounding and im-portant personages. But, either from boyish curiosity or some sense of being mis-understood, Clarence was more attracted by the two individuals of the party who were least kind to him—namely, Mrs. Peyton and her brother Harry. I fear that, after the fashion of most children, and some grown-up people, he thought less of the steady kindness of Mr. Peyton and the others than of the rare tolerance of Harry or the polite concessions of his sister. Miserably conscious of this at times, he quite convinced himself that if he could only win a word of approbation from Harry, or a smile from Mrs. Peyton, he would afterwards revenge himself by "running away." Whether he would or not, I cannot say. I am writing of a foolish, growing, impres-sionable boy of eleven, of whose sentiments nothing could be safely predicted but uncertainty.

It was at this time that he became fascinated by another member of the party, whose position had been too humble and unimportant to be included in the group already noted. Of the same appearance as the other teamsters in size, habits, and apparel, he had not at first exhibited to Clarence any claim to sympathy. But it appeared that he was actually a youth of only sixteen—a hopeless incorrigible of St. Joseph, whose parents had prevailed on Peyton to allow him to join the party, by way of removing him from evil associations and as a method of reform. Of this Clarence was at first ignorant, not from any want of frankness on the part of the youth, for that ingenious young gentleman later informed him that he had killed three men in St. Louis, two in St. Jo, and that the officers of justice were after him. But it was evident that to precocious habits of drinking, smoking, chewing, and card-playing this overgrown youth added a strong tendency to exaggeration of statement. Indeed, he was known as "Lying Jim Hooker," and his various qualities presented a problem to Clarence that was attractive and inspiring, doubtful, but always fascinating. "With the hoarse voice of early wickedness and a contempt for ordinary courtesy, he had a round, perfectly good-humored face, and a disposition that, when not called upon to act up to his self-imposed rôle of reckless wickedness, was not unkindly.

It was only a few days after the massacre, and while the children were still wrapped in the gloomy interest and frightened reticence which followed it, that "Jim Hooker" first characteristically flashed upon Clarence's perceptions. Hanging half on and half off the saddle of an Indian pony, the lank Jim suddenly made his appearance, dashing violently up and down the track, and around the wagon in which Clarence was sitting, tugging desperately at the reins, with every indication of being furiously run away with, and retaining his seat only with the most dauntless courage and skill. Round and round they went, the helpless rider at times hanging by a single stirrup near the ground, and again recovering himself by—as it seemed to Clarence almost superhuman effort. Clarence sat open-mouthed with anxiety and excitement, and yet a few of the other teamsters laughed. Then the voice of Mr. Peyton, from the window of his car, said quietly,—

"There, that will do, Jim. Quit it!"

The furious horse and rider instantly disappeared. A few moments after, the bewildered Clarence saw the redoubted horseman trotting along quietly in the dust of the rear, on the same fiery steed, who in that prosaic light bore an astounding resemblance to an ordinary team horse. Later in the day he sought an explanation from the rider.

"You see," answered Jim gloomily, "thar ain't a galoot in this yer crowd ez knows jist *what's* in that hoss! And them ez suspecks daren't say! It wouldn't do for to hev it let out that the Judge hez a Morgan-Mexican plug that's killed two men afore he got him, and is bound to kill another afore he gets through! Why, on'y the week afore we kem up to you, that thar hoss bolted with me at camping! Bucked and throwed me, but I kept my holt o' the stirrups with my foot—so! Dragged me a matter of two miles, head down, and me keepin' away rocks with, my hand—so!"

"Why didn't you loose your foot and let go?" asked Clarence breathlessly.

"*You* might," said Jim, with deep scorn; "that ain't *my* style. I just laid low till we kern to a steep pitched hill, and goin' down when the hoss was, so to speak, kinder *below* me, I just turned a hand spring, so, and that landed me onter his back again."

This action, though vividly illustrated by Jim's throwing Ins hands down like feet beneath him, and indicating the parabola of a spring in the air, proving altogether too much for Clarence's mind to grasp, he timidly turned to a less difficult detail.

"What made the horse bolt first, Mr. Hooker?"

"Smelt Injins!" said Jim, carelessly expectorating tobacco juice in a curving jet from the side of his mouth—a singularly fascinating accomplishment, peculiarly ins own, " 'n' likely *your* Injins."

"But," argued Clarence hesitatingly, "you said it was a week before—and"—

"Er Mexican plug kin smell Injins fifty, yes, a hundred miles away," said Jim, with scornful deliberation; " 'n' if Judge Peyton had took my advice, and hadn't been so mighty feared about the character of his hoss gettin' out, he 'd hev played roots on them Injins afore they tetched ye. But," he added, with gloomy dejection, "there ain't no sand in this yer crowd, thar ain't no vim, thar ain't nothin'; and thar kan't be ez long ez thar's women and babies, and women and baby fixin's, mixed up with it. I'd hev cut the whole blamed gang ef it weren't for one or two things," he added darkly.

Clarence, impressed by Jim's mysterious manner, for the moment forgot his contemptuous allusion to Mr. Peyton, and the evident implication of Susy and himself, and asked hurriedly, "What things?"

Jim, as if forgetful of the boy's presence in his fitful mood, abstractedly half drew a glittering bowie knife from his boot leg, and then slowly put it back again. "Thar's one or two old scores," he continued, in a low voice, although no one was in hearing distance of them "one or two private accounts," he went on tragically, averting his eyes as if watched by some one, "thet hev to be wiped out with blood afore *I* leave. Thar's one or two men *too many* alive and breathin' in this yer crowd. Mebbee it's Gus Gildersleeve; mebbee it's Harry Benham; mebbee," he added, with dark yet noble disinterestedness, "it's *me*."

"Oh, no, said Clarence, with polite deprecation.

Far from placating the gloomy Jim, this seemed only to awake his suspicions. "Mebbee," he said, dancing suddenly away from Clarence, "mebbee you think I'm lyin' Mebbee you think, because you're Colonel Brant's son, yer kin run *me* with this yer train. Mebbee," he continued, dancing violently back again, "ye kalkilate, because ye run off 'n' stampeded a baby, ye kin tote me round too, sonny. Mebbee," he went on, executing a double shuffle in the dust, and alternately striking his hands on the sides of his boots, "mebbee you're spyin' round and reportin' to the Judge."

Firmly convinced that Jim was working himself up by an Indian war-dance to some desperate assault on himself, but resenting the last unjust accusation, Clarence had recourse to one of his old dogged silences. Happily at this moment an authoritative voice called out, "Now, then, you Jim Hooker!" and the desperate Hooker, as usual, vanished instantly. Nevertheless, he appeared an hour or two later beside the wagon in which Susy and Clarence were with an expression of satiated vengeance and remorseful blood guiltiness in his face, and his hair combed Indian fashion over his eyes. As he generously contented himself with only passing a gloomy and disparaging criticism on the game of cards that the children were playing, it struck Clarence, for the first time that a great deal of his real wickedness resided in his hair. This set him to thinking that it was strange that Mr. Peyton did not try to reform him with a pair of scissors, but not until Clarence himself had for at least four days attempted to imitate Jim by combing his own hair in that fashion.

A few days later, Jim again casually favored him with a confidential interview. Clarence had been allowed to bestride one of the team leaders postillionwise, and was correspondingly elevated, when Jim joined him, on the Mexican plug, which appeared—no doubt a part of its wicked art—heavily docile, and even slightly lame.

"How much," said Jim, in a tone of gloomy confidence,—"how much did you reckon to make by stealin' that gal-baby, sonny?"

"Nothing," replied Clarence, with a smile. Perhaps it was an evidence of the marked influence that Jim was beginning to exert over him that he already did not attempt to resent this fascinating implication of grownup guilt.

"It orter bin a good job, if it warn't revenge, continued Jim moodily.

"No, it wasn't revenge," said Clarence hurriedly.

"Then ye kalkilated ter get er hundred dollars reward ef the old man and old woman hadn't bin scelped afore ye got up to 'em?" said Jim "That' your blamed dodgasted luck, eh! Enyhow, you'll make Mrs. Peyton plank down suthin' if she adopts the babby. Look yer, young feller," he said, starting suddenly and, throwing his face forward, glaring fiendishly through his matted side-locks, "d' ye mean ter tell me it wasn't a plant—a skin game—the hull thing?"

"A what?" said Clarence.

"D' ye mean to say"—it was wonderful how gratuitously husky his voice became at this moment—"d' ye mean ter tell *me* ye didn't set on them Injins to wipe out the Silsbees, so that ye could hev an out-an'-out gal *orfen* on hand fer Mrs. Peyton ter adopt—eh?"

But here Clarence was forced to protest, and strongly, although Jim contemptuously ignored it. "Don't lie ter me," he repeated mysteriously, "I'm fly. I'm dark, young fel. We're cahoots in this thing?" And with this artful suggestion of being in possession of Clarence's guilty secret, he departed in time to elude the usual objurgation of his superior, "Phil," the head teamster.

Nor was his baleful fascination exercised entirely on Clarence. In spite of Mrs. Peyton's jealously affectionate care, Clarence's frequent companionship, and the little circle of admiring courtiers that always surrounded Susy, it became evident that this small Eve had been secretly approached and tempted by the Satanic Jim. She was found one day to have a few heron's feathers in her possession with which she adorned her curls, and at another time was discovered to have rubbed her face and arms with yellow and red ochre, confessedly the free gift of Jim Hooker. It was to Clarence alone that she admitted the significance and purport of these offerings. "Jim gave 'em to me," she said, "and Jim's a kind of Injin hisself that won't hurt me; and when bad Injins come, they'll think I'm his Injin baby and run away. And Jim said if I'd just told the Injins, when they came to kill papa and mamma, that I b'longed to him, they'd hev runned away."

"But," said, the practical Clarence, "you could not; you know you were with Mrs. Peyton all the time."

"Kla'uns," said, Susy, shaking her head and fixing her round blue eyes with calm mendacity on the boy, "don't you tell me. *I was there!*"

Clarence started back, and nearly fell over the wagon in hopeless dismay at this dreadful revelation of Susy's powers of exaggeration. "But," he gasped, "you know, Susy, you and me left before"—

"Kla'uns," said Susy calmly, making a little pleat in the skirt of her dress with her small thumb and fingers, "don't you talk to me. I was there. I'se a *seriver!* The men at the fort said so! The *serivers* is allus, allus there, and allus, allus knows everythin'."

Clarence was too dumfounded to reply. He had a vague recollection of having noticed before that Susy was very much fascinated by the reputation given to her at Fort Ridge as a "survivor," and was trying in an infantile way to live up to it. This the wicked Jim had evidently encouraged. For a day or two Clarence felt a little afraid of her, and more lonely than ever.

It was in this state, and while he was doggedly conscious that his association with Jim did not prepossess Mrs. Peyton or her brother in his favor, and that the former even believed him responsible for Susy's unhallowed acquaintance with Jim, that he drifted into one of those youthful escapades on which elders are apt to sit in severe but not always considerate judgment. Believing, like many other children, that nobody cared particularly for him, except to *restrain* him, discovering, as children do, much sooner than we complacently imagine, that love and preference have no logical connection with desert or character, Clarence became boyishly reckless. But when, one day, it was rumored that a herd of buffalo was in the vicinity, and that the train would be delayed the next rooming in order that a hunt might be organized by Gildersleeve, Benham, and a few others, Clarence listened willingly to Jim's proposition that they should secretly follow it.

To effect their unhallowed purpose required boldness and duplicity. It was arranged that shortly after the departure of the hunting party Clarence should ask permission to mount and exercise one of the team horses—a favor that had been frequently granted him; that in the outskirts of the camp he should pretend that the horse ran away with him, and Jim would start in pursuit. The absence of the shooting party with so large a contingent of horses and men would preclude any further detachment from the camp to assist them. Once clear, they would follow the track of the hunters, and, if discovered by them, would offer the same excuse, with the addition that they had lost their way to the camp. The plan was successful. The details were carried out with almost too perfect effect; as it appeared that Jim, in order to give dramatic intensity to the fractiousness of Clarence's horse, had inserted a thorn apple under the neck of his saddle, which Clarence only discovered in time to prevent himself from being unseated. Urged forward by ostentatious "Whoas!" and surreptitious cuts in the rear from Jim, pursuer and pursued presently found themselves safely beyond the half-dry stream and fringe of alder bushes that Skirted the camp. They were not followed. Whether the teamsters suspected and winked at this design, or believed that the boys could take care of themselves, and ran no risk of being lost in the proximity of the hunting party, there was no general alarm.

Thus reassured, and having a general idea of the direction of the hunt, the boys pushed hilariously forward. Before them opened a vast expanse of bottom land, slightly sloping on the right to a distant half-filled lagoon, formed by the main river overflow, on whose tributary they had encamped. The lagoon was partly hidden by straggling timber and "brush," and beyond that, again, stretched the unlimitable plains—the pasture of their mighty game. Hither, Jim hoarsely informed his companion, the buffaloes came to water. A few rods further on, he started dramatically, and, alighting, proceeded to slowly examine the ground. It seemed to be scattered over with half-circular patches, which he pointed out mysteriously as "buffalo chip." To Clarence's inexperienced perception the plain, bore a singular resemblance to the surface of an ordinary unromantic cattle pasture that somewhat chilled his heroic fancy. However, the two companions halted and professionally examined their arms and equipments.

These, I grieve to say, though varied, were scarcely full or satisfactory. The necessities of their flight had restricted Jim to an old double-barreled fowling-piece, which he usually carried slung across ins shoulders; an old-fashioned "six-shooter," whose barrels revolved occasionally and unexpectedly, known as "Allen's Pepper

Box" on account of its culinary resemblance; and a bowie- knife. Clarence carried an Indian bow and arrow with which he had been exercising, and a hatchet which he had concealed under the flanks of his saddle. To this Jim generously added the six-shooter, taking the hatchet in exchange—a transfer that at first delighted Clarence, until, seeing the warlike and picturesque effect of the hatchet in Jim's belt, he regretted, the transfer. The gun, Jim meantime explained, "extry charged," "chuck up" to the middle with slugs and revolver bullets, could only be fired by himself, and even then, he darkly added, not without danger. This poverty of equipment was, however, compensated by opposite statements from Jim of the extraordinary results obtained by these simple weapons from "fellers I knew:" how *he* himself had once brought down a bull by a bold shot with a revolver through its open bellowing mouth that pierced its "innards;" How a friend of his—an intimate in fact—now in jail at Louisville for killing a sheriff's deputy, had once found himself alone and dismounted with a simple clasp-knife and a lariat among a herd of buffaloes; how, leaping calmly upon the shaggy shoulders of the biggest bull, he lashed himself with the lariat firmly to its horns, goading it onward with his clasp-knife, and subsisting for days upon the flesh cut from its living body, until, abandoned by its fellows, and exhausted by loss of blood, it finally succumbed to its victor at the very outskirts of the camp to which he had artfully driven it! It must be confessed that this recital somewhat took away Clarence's breath, and he would have liked to ask a few questions. But they were alone on the prairie, and linked by a common transgression; the glorious sun was coming up victoriously, the pure, crisp air was intoxicating their nerves; in the bright forecast of youth everything *was* possible!

The surface of the bottom land that they were crossing was here and there broken up by fissures and "pot-holes," and some circumspection in their progress became necessary. In one of these halts, Clarence was struck by a dull, monotonous jarring that sounded like the heavy, regular fall of water over a dam. Each time that they slackened their pace the sound would become more audible, and was at last accompanied by that slight but unmistakable tremor of the earth that betrayed the vicinity of a waterfall. Hesitating over this phenomenon, which seemed to imply that their topography was wrong and that they had blundered from the track, they were presently startled by the fact that the sound was actually *approaching* them! With a sudden instinct they both galloped towards the lagoon. As the timber opened before them Jim uttered a long ecstatic shout: Why, it's ***them!***"

At a first glance it seemed to Clarence as if the whole plain beyond was broken up and rolling in tumbling waves or furrows towards them. A second glance showed the tossing fronts of a vast herd of buffaloes, and here and there, darting in and out and among them, or emerging from the cloud of dust behind, wild figures and flashes of fire. With the idea of water still in his mind, it seemed as if some tumultuous tidal wave were sweeping unseen towards the lagoon, carrying everything before it. He turned with eager eyes, in speechless expectancy, to his companion.

Alack! that redoutable hero and mighty hunter was, to all appearances, equally speechless and astonished. It was true that he remained rooted to the saddle, a lank, still heroic figure, alternately grasping his hatchet and gun with a kind of spasmodic regularity. How long he would have continued this could, never be known, for the next moment, with a deafening crash, the herd broke through the brush, and, swerving at the right of the lagoon, bore down directly upon them. All further doubt or hesitation on their part was stopped. The far-seeing, sagacious Mexican plug with a terrific snort wheeled and fled furiously with his rider. Moved, no doubt, by touching fidelity, Clarence's humbler team-horse instantly followed. In a few moments those devoted animals struggled neck to neck in noble emulation.

"What are we goin' oil this way for?" gasped the simple Clarence.

"Peyton and Gildersleeve are back there—and they'll see us," gasped Jim in reply. It struck Clarence that the buffaloes were much nearer them than the hunting party, and that the trampling hoofs of a dozen bulls were close behind them, but with another gasp he shouted,

"When are we going to hunt 'em?

"Hunt ***them!***" screamed Jim, with a hysterical outburst of truth; "why, they're huntin' ***us***—dash it!"

Indeed, there was no doubt that their frenzied horses were flying before the equally frenzied herd behind them. They gained a momentary advantage by riding into one of the fissures, and out again on the other side, while their pursuers were obliged to make a detour. But in a few minutes they were overtaken by that part of the herd who had taken the other and nearer side of the lagoon, and were now fairly in the midst of them. The ground shook with their trampling hoofs; their steaming breath, mingling with, the stinging dust that filled the air, half choked and blinded Clarence. He was dimly conscious that Jim had wildly thrown his hatchet at a cow-buffalo pressing close upon his flanks. As they swept down into another gully he saw him raise his fateful gun in utter desperation. Clarence crouched low on his horse's outstretched neck. There was a, blinding flash, a single stunning report from both barrels; Jim reeled in one way half out of the saddle, while the smoking gun seemed to leap in another over his head, and then rider and horse vanished in a choking cloud of dust and gunpowder. A moment after Clarence's horse stopped with a sudden check, and the boy felt himself hurled over its head into the gully, alighting on something that seemed to be a bounding cushion of curled and twisted hair. It was the shaggy shoulder of an enormous buffalo! For Jim's desperate random shot and double charge had taken effect on the near hind leg of a preceding bull, tearing away the flesh and ham-stringing the animal, who had dropped in the gully just in front of Clarence's horse.

Dazed but unhurt, the boy rolled from the lifted fore quarters of the struggling brute to the ground. When he staggered to his feet again, not only his horse was gone, but the whole herd of buffaloes seemed to have passed too, and he could hear the shouts of unseen hunters now ahead of him. They had evidently overlooked his fall, and the gully had concealed him. The sides before him were too steep for his aching limbs to climb; the slope by which he and the bull had descended when the collision occurred was behind the wounded animal. Clarence was staggering towards it when the bull, by a supreme effort, lifted itself on three legs, half turned, and faced him.

These events had passed too quickly for the inexperienced boy to have felt any active fear, or indeed anything but wild excitement and confusion. But the spectacle of that shaggy and enormous front, that seemed to fill the whole gully, rising with awful deliberation between him and escape, sent a thrill of terror through his frame. The great, dull, bloodshot eyes glared at him with a dumb, wondering fury; the large wet nostrils were so near that their first snort of inarticulate rage made him reel backwards as from a blow. The gully was only a narrow and short fissure or subsidence of the plain; a few paces more of retreat and he would be at its end, against an almost perpendicular bank fifteen feet high. If he attempted to climb its crumbling sides and fell, there would be those short but terrible horns waiting to impale him! It seemed too terrible, too cruel! He was so small beside this overgrown monster. It wasn't fair! The tears started to his eye, and then, in a rage at the injustice of Fate, he stood doggedly still with clenched fists. He fixed his gaze with half-hysterical, childish fury on those lurid eyes; he did not know that, owing to the strange magnifying power of the bull's convex pupils, he, Clarence, appeared much bigger than he really was to the brute's heavy consciousness, the distance from him most deceptive, and that it was to this fact that hunters so often owed their escape. He only thought of some desperate means of attack. Ah! the six-shooter. It was still in his pocket. He drew it nervously, hopelessly—it looked so small compared with his large enemy!

He presented it with flashing eyes, and pulled the trigger. A feeble click followed, another, and again! Even *this* had mocked him. He pulled the trigger once more, wildly; there was a sudden explosion, and another. He stepped back; the balls had apparently flattened themselves harmlessly on the bull's forehead. He pulled again, hopelessly; there was another report, a sudden furious bellow, and the enormous brute threw his head savagely to one side, burying his left horn deep in the crumbling bank beside him. Again and again he charged the bank, driving his left horn home, and bringing down the stones and earth in showers. It was some seconds before Clarence saw in a single glimpse of that wildly tossing crest the reason of this fury. The blood was pouring from his left eye, penetrated by the last bullet; the bull was blinded! A terrible revulsion of feeling, a sudden sense of remorse that was for the moment more awful than even his previous fear, overcame him. *He* had done *that thing!* As much to fly from the dreadful spectacle as any instinct of self-preservation, he took advantage of the next mad paroxysms of pain and blindness, that always impelled the suffering beast towards the left, to slip past him on the right, reach the incline, and scramble wildly up to the plain again. Here he ran confusedly forward, not knowing whither—only caring to escape that agonized bellowing, to shut out forever the accusing look of that huge blood-weltering eye.

Suddenly he heard a distant angry shout. To his first hurried glance the plain had seemed empty, but, looking up, he saw two horsemen rapidly advancing with a led horse behind them—his own. With the blessed sense of relief that overtook him now came the fevered desire for sympathy and to tell them all. But as they came nearer he saw that they were Gildersleeve, the scout, and Henry Benham, and that, far from sharing any delight m his deliverance, their faces only exhibited irascible impatience. Overcome by this new defeat, the boy stopped, again dumb and dogged.

"Now, then, blank it all, *will* you get up and come along, or do you reckon to keep the train waiting another hour over your blanked foolishness?" said Gildersleeve savagely.

The boy hesitated, and then mounted mechanically, without a word.

"'T would have served 'em right to have gone and left 'em," muttered Benham vindictively.

For one wild instant Clarence thought of throwing himself from his horse and bidding them go on and leave him. But before he could put this thought into action the two men were galloping forward, with his horse led by a lariat fastened to the horn of Gildersleeve's saddle.

In two hours more they had overtaken the train, already on the march, and were in the midst of the group of outriders. Judge Peyton's face, albeit a trifle perplexed, turned towards Clarence with a kindly, half-tolerant look of welcome. The boy's heart instantly melted with forgiveness.

"Well, my boy, let's hear *your* story. What happened?"

Clarence cast a hurried glance around, and saw Jim, with face averted, riding gloomily behind. Then nervously and hurriedly he told how he had been thrown into the gully on the back of the wounded buffalo, and the manner of his escape. An audible titter ran through the cavalcade. Mr. Peyton regarded him gravely. "But how did the buffalo get so conveniently into the gully? he asked.

"Jim Hooker lamed him with a shotgun, and he fell over," said Clarence timidly.

A roar of Homeric laughter went up from the party. Clarence looked up, stung and startled, but caught a single glimpse of Jim Hooker's face that made him forget his own mortification. In its hopeless, heart-sick, and utterly beaten dejection— the first and only real expression he had seen on it—he read the dreadful truth. Jim's *reputation* had ruined him! The one genuine and striking episode of his life, the one trustworthy account he had given of it, had been unanimously accepted as the biggest and most consummate lie of his record!

CHAPTER VII.

WITH this incident of the hunt closed, to Clarence, the last remembered episode of his journey. But he did not know until long after that it had also closed to him what might have been the opening of a new career. For it had been Judge Peyton's intention in adopting Susy to include a certain guardianship and protection of me boy, provided he could get the consent of that vague relation to whom he was consigned. But it had been pointed out by Mrs. Peyton and her brother that Clarence's association with Jim Hooker had made him a doubtful companion for Susy, and even the Judge himself was forced to admit that the boy's apparent taste for evil company was inconsistent with his alleged birth and breeding. Unfortunately, Clarence, in the conviction of being hopelessly misunderstood, and that dogged acquiescence to fate which was one of his characteristics, was too proud to correct the impression by any of me hypocrisies of childhood. He had also a cloudy instinct of loyalty to Jim in his disgrace, without, however, experiencing either the sympathy of an equal or the zeal of a partisan, but rather—if it could be said of a boy of his years—with the patronage and protection of a superior. So he accepted without demur the intimation that when the train reached California he would be forwarded from Stockton with an outfit and a letter of explanation to Sacramento, it being understood that in the event of not finding his relative he would return to the Peytons in one of the southern valleys, where they elected to purchase a tract of land.

With this outlook, and the prospect of change, independence, and all the rich possibilities that to the imagination of youth are included in them, Clarence had found the days dragging. The halt at Salt Lake, the transit of the dreary Alkali desert, even the wild passage of the Sierras, were but a blurred picture in his memory. The sight of eternal snows and the rolling of endless ranks of pines, the first glimpse of a hillside of wild oats, the spectacle of a rushing yellow river that to his fancy seemed tinged with gold, were momentary excitements, quickly forgotten. But when, one morning, halting at the outskirts of a struggling settlement, he found the entire party eagerly gathered around a passing stranger, who had taken from his saddle-bags a small buckskin pouch to show them a double handful of shining scales of metal,

Clarence, felt the first feverish and overmastering thrill of the gold-seekers. Breathlessly he followed the breathless questions and careless replies. The gold had been dug out of a *placer* only thirty miles away. It might be worth, say, a hundred and fifty dollars; it was only *his* share of a week's work with two partners. It was not much; "the country was getting played out with fresh arrivals and greenhorns." All this falling carelessly from the unshaven lips of a dusty, roughly dressed man, with a long-handled shovel and pickaxe strapped on his back, and a frying-pan depending from his saddle. But no panoplied or armed knight ever seemed so heroic or independent a figure to Clarence. What could be finer than the noble scorn conveyed in his critical survey of the train, with its comfortable covered wagons and appliances of civilization? "Ye'll hev to get rid of them ther fixin's if yer goin' in for *placer* diggin'!" What a corroboration of Clarence's real thoughts! What a picture of independence was this! The picturesque scout, the all - powerful Judge Peyton, the daring young officer, all crumbled on their clayey pedestals before this hero in a red flannel shirt and high-topped boots. To stroll around in the open air all day, and pick up those shining bits of metal, without study, without method or routine—this was really life; to some day come upon that large nugget "you couldn't lift," that was worth as much as the train and horses—such a one as the stranger said was found the other day at Sawyer's Bar—this was worth giving up everything for. That rough man, with his smile of careless superiority, was the living link between Clarence and the Thousand and One Nights; in him were Aladdin and Sinbad incarnate.

Two days later they reached Stockton. Here Clarence, whose single suit of clothes had been reinforced by patching, odds and ends from Peyton's stores, and an extraordinary costume of army cloth, got up by the regimental tailor of Fort Ridge, was taken to be refitted at a general furnishing "emporium." But alas! in the selection of the clothing for that adult locality scant provision seemed to have been made for a boy of Clarence's years, and he was with difficulty fitted from an old condemned Government stores with "a boy's" seaman suit and a brass - buttoned pea-jacket. To this outfit Mr. Peyton added a small sum of money for his expenses, and a letter of explanation to his cousin. The stage-coach was to start at noon. It only remained for Clarence to take leave of the party. The final parting with Susy had been discounted on the two previous days with some tears, small frights and clingings, and the expressed determination on the child's part "to go with him;" but in the excitement of the arrival at Stockton it was still further mitigated, and under the influence of a little present from Clarence—his first disbursement of his small capital—had at last taken the form and promise of merely temporary separation. Nevertheless, when the boy's scanty pack was deposited under the stage-coach seat, and he had been left alone, he ran rapidly back to the train for one moment more with Susy. Panting and a little frightened, he reached Mrs. Peyton's car.

"Goodness! You're not gone yet," said Mrs. Peyton sharply. "Do you want to lose the stage?"

An instant before, in his loneliness, he might have answered, "Yes." But under the cruel sting of Mrs. Peyton's evident annoyance at his reappearance he felt his legs suddenly tremble, and his voice left him. He did not dare to look at Susy. But her voice rose comfortably from the depths of the wagon where she was sitting.

"The stage will be goned away, Kla'uns."

She too! Shame at his foolish weakness sent the yearning blood that had settled round his heart flying back into his face.

"I was looking for—for—for Jim, ma'am," he said at last, boldly.

He saw a look of disgust pass over Mrs. Peyton's face, and felt a malicious satisfaction as he turned and ran back to the stage. But here, to his surprise, he actually found Jim, whom he really hadn't thought of, darkly watching the last strapping of luggage. With a manner calculated to convey the impression to the other passengers that he was parting from a brother criminal, probably on his way to a state prison, Jim shook hands gloomily with Clarence, and eyed the other passengers furtively between his matted locks.

"Ef ye hear o' anythin' happenin', ye'll know what's up," he said, in a low, hoarse, but perfectly audible whisper. "Me and them's bound to part company afore long. Tell the fellows at Deadman's Gulch to look out for me at any time."

Although Clarence was not going to Deadman's Gulch, knew nothing of it, and had a faint suspicion that Jim was equally ignorant, yet as one or two of the passengers glanced anxiously at the demure, gray-eyed boy who seemed booked for such a baleful destination, he really felt the half-delighted, half-frightened consciousness that he was starting in life under fascinating immoral pretenses. But the forward spring of the fine-spirited horses, the quickened motion, the glittering sunlight, and the thought that he really was leaving behind him all the shackles of dependence and custom, and plunging into a life of freedom, drove all else from his mind. He turned at last from this hopeful, blissful future, and began to examine his fellow-passengers with boyish curiosity. Wedged in between two silent men on the front seat, one of whom seemed a farmer, and the other, by his black attire, a professional man, Clarence was finally attracted by a black-mantled, dark-haired, bonnetless woman on the back seat, whose attention seemed, to be monopolized, by the jocular gallantries of her companions and the two men before her in the middle seat. From her position he could see little more than her dark eyes, which occasionally seemed to meet his frank curiosity in an amused sort of way, but he was chiefly struck by the pretty foreign sound of her musical voice, which was unlike anything he had ever heard before, and—alas for the inconstancy of youth—much finer than Mrs. Peyton's. Presently his farmer companion, casting a patronizing glance on Clarence's pea-jacket and brass buttons, said cheerily—

"Jest off a voyage, sonny?"

"No, sir," stammered Clarence; "I came across the plains."

"Then I reckon that's the rig-out for the crew of a prairie schooner, eh?" There was a laugh at this which perplexed Clarence. Observing it, the humorist kindly condescended to explain that "prairie schooner" was the current slang for an emigrant wagon.

"I couldn't," explained. Clarence, naively looking at the dark eyes on the back seat, "get any clothes at Stockton but these; I suppose the folks didn't think there'd ever be boys in California." The simplicity of this speech evidently impressed the others, for the two men in the middle seats turned at a whisper from the lady and regarded him curiously. Clarence blushed slightly and became silent. Presently the vehicle began to slacken its speed. They were ascending a hill; on either bank grew huge cottonwoods, from which occasionally depended a beautiful scarlet vine.

"Ah! eet ees pretty," said the lady, nodding her black-veiled head towards it. "Eet is good in ze hair."

One of the men made an awkward attempt to clutch a spray from the window. A brilliant inspiration flashed upon Clarence. When the stage began the ascent of the next hill, following the example of an outside passenger, he jumped down to walk. At the top of the hill he rejoined the stage, flushed and panting, but carrying a small branch of the vine in his scratched hands. Handing it to the man on the middle seat, he said, with grave, boyish politeness—"Please—for the lady."

A slight smile passed over the face of Clarence's neighbors. The bonnetless woman nodded a pleasant acknowledgment, and coquettishly wound the vine in her glossy hair. The dark man at his side, who hadn't spoken yet, turned to Clarence dryly.

"If you're goin' to keep up this gait, sonny, I reckon ye won't find much trouble gettin' a man's suit to fit you by the time you reach Sacramento."

Clarence didn't quite understand him, but noticed that a singular gravity seemed to overtake the two jocular men on the middle seat, and the lady looked out of the window. He came to the conclusion that he had made a mistake about alluding to his clothes and his size. He must try and behave more manly. That opportunity seemed to be offered two hours later, when the stage stopped at a wayside hotel or restaurant.

Two or three passengers had got down to refresh themselves at the bar. His right and left hand neighbors were, however, engaged in a drawling conversation on the comparative merits of San Francisco sand-hill and water lots; the jocular occupants of the middle seat were still engrossed with the lady. Clarence slipped out of the stage and entered the bar-room with some ostentation. The complete ignoring of his person by the barkeeper and his customers, however, somewhat disconcerted him. He hesitated a moment, and then returned gravely to the stage door and opened it.

"Would you mind taking a drink with me, sir?" said Clarence politely, addressing the farmer-looking passenger who had been most civil to him. A dead silence followed. The two men on the middle seat faced entirely around to gaze at him.

"The Commodore asks if you'll take a drink with him," explained one of the men to Clarence's friend with the greatest seriousness.

"Eh? Oh, yes, certainly," returned that gentleman, changing his astonished expression to one of the deepest gravity, "seeing it's the Commodore."

"And perhaps you and your friend will join, too?" said Clarence timidly to the passenger who had explained; "and you too, sir? he added to the dark man.

"Really, gentlemen, I don't see how we can refuse," said the latter, with the greatest formality, and appealing to the others. "A compliment of this kind from our distinguished friend is not to be taken lightly."

"I have observed, sir, that the Commodore's head is level," returned the other man with equal gravity.

Clarence could have wished they had not treated his first hospitable effort quite so formally, but as they stepped from the coach with unbending faces he led them, a little frightened, into the bar-room. Here, unfortunately, as he was barely able to reach over the counter, the barkeeper would have again overlooked him but for a quick glance from the dark man, which seemed to change even the barkeeper's perfunctory smiling face into supernatural gravity.

"The Commodore is standing treat," said the dark man, with unbroken seriousness, indicating Clarence, and leaning back with an air of respectful formality. "*I* will take straight whiskey. The Commodore, on account of just changing climate, will, I believe, for the present content himself with lemon soda."

Clarence had previously resolved to take whiskey, like the others, but a little doubtful of the politeness of countermanding his guest's order, and perhaps slightly embarrassed by the fact that all the other customers seemed to have gathered round him and his party with equally immovable faces, he said hurriedly,

"Lemon soda for me, please."

"The Commodore," said the barkeeper, with impassive features, as he bent forward and wiped the counter with professional deliberation, "is right. No matter how much a man may be accustomed all his life to liquor, when he is changing climate, gentlemen, he says 'Lemon soda for me' all the time."

"Perhaps," said Clarence, brightening, "you will join too?"

"I shall be proud on this occasion, sir."

"I think," said the tall man, still as ceremoniously unbending as before, "that there can be but one toast here, gentlemen. I give you the health of the Commodore. May his shadow never be less."

The health was drunk solemnly. Clarence felt his cheeks tingle, and in his excitement drank his own health with the others. Yet he was disappointed that there was not more joviality; he wondered if men always drank together so stiffly. And it occurred to him that it would be expensive. Nevertheless, he had his purse all ready ostentatiously in his hand; in fact, the paying for it out of his own money was not the least manly and independent pleasure he had promised himself. "How much?" he asked, with an affectation of carelessness.

The barkeeper cast ms eye professionally over the bar-room. "I think you said treats for the crowd; call it twenty dollars to make even change."

Clarence's heart sank. He had heard already of the exaggeration of California prices. Twenty dollars! It was half his fortune. Nevertheless, with an heroic effort, he controlled himself, and with slightly nervous fingers counted out the money. It struck him, however, as curious, not to say ungentlemanly, that the bystanders craned their necks over his shoulder to look at the contents of his purse, although some slight explanation was offered by the tall man.

"The Commodore's purse, gentlemen, is really a singular one. Permit me," he said, taking it from Clarence's hand with great politeness. "It is one of the new pattern, you observe, quite worthy of inspection." He handed it to a man behind him, who m turn handed it to another, while a chorus of "suthin quite new," "the latest style," followed it in its passage round the room, and indicated to Clarence its whereabouts. It was presently handed back to the barkeeper, who had begged also to inspect it, and who, with an air of scrupulous ceremony, insisted upon placing it himself in Clarence's side pocket, as if it were an important part of his function. The driver here called "all aboard." The passengers hurriedly reseated themselves, and the episode abruptly ended. For, to Clarence's surprise, these attentive friends of a moment ago at once became interested in the views of a new passenger concerning the local politics of San Francisco, and he found himself utterly forgotten. The bonnetless woman had changed her position, and her head was no longer visible. The disillusion and depression that overcame him suddenly were as complete as his previous expectations and hopefulness had been extravagant. For the first time his utter unimportance in the world and his inadequacy to this new life around him came upon him crushingly.

The heat and jolting of the stage caused him to fall into a slight slumber, and when he awoke he found his two neighbors had just got out at a wayside station. They had evidently not cared to waken him to say "Good-by." From the conversation of the other passengers he learned that the tall man was a well-known gambler, and the one who looked like a farmer was a ship captain who had become a wealthy merchant. Clarence thought he understood now why the latter had asked him if he came oil a voyage, and that the nickname of "Commodore" given to him, Clarence, was some joke intended for the captain's understanding. He missed them, for he

wanted to talk to them about his relative at Sacramento, whom he was now so soon
to see. At last, between sleeping and waking, the end of his journey was unexpectedly reached. It was dark, but, being "steamer night," the shops and business places
were still open, and Mr. Peyton had arranged that the stage-driver should deliver
Clarence at the address of his relative in "J Street,"—an address which Clarence had
luckily remembered. But the boy was somewhat discomfited to find that it was a
large office or banking-house. He, however, descended from the stage, and with his
small pack m his hand entered the building as the stage drove off, and, addressing
one of the busy clerks, asked for "Mr. Jackson Brant."

There was no such person in the office. There never had been any such person.
The bank had always occupied that building. Was there not some mistake in the
number? No; the name, number, and street had been deeply engrafted in the boy's
recollection. Stop! it might be the name of a customer who had given his address at
the bank. The clerk who made this suggestion disappeared promptly to make inqui-
ries in the counting-room. Clarence, with a rapidly beating heart, awaited him. The
clerk returned. There was no such name on the books. Jackson Brant was utterly
unknown to every one in the establishment.

For an instant the counter against which the boy was leaning seemed to yield
with his weight; he was obliged to steady himself with both hands to keep from
falling. It was not his disappointment, which was terrible; it was not a thought of
his future, which seemed hopeless; it was not his injured pride at appearing to have
willfully deceived Mr. Peyton, which was more dreadful than all these; but it was
the sudden, sickening sense that *he* himself had been deceived, tricked, and fooled!
For it Hashed upon him for the first time that the vague sense of wrong which had
always haunted him was this—that this was the vile culmination of a plan to *get
rid of him,* and that he had been deliberately lost and led astray by his relatives as
helplessly and completely as a useless cat or dog!

Perhaps there was something of this in his face, for the clerk, staring at him,
bade him sit down for a moment, and again vanished into the mysterious interior.
Clarence had no conception how long he was absent, or indeed of anything but his
own breathless thoughts, for he was conscious of wondering afterwards why the
clerk was leading him through a door in the counter into an inner room of many
desks, and again through a glass door into a smaller office, where a preternaturally

busy-looking man sat writing at a desk. Without looking up, but pausing only to apply a blotting-pad to the paper before him, the man said crisply—

"So you've been consigned to some one who don't seem to turn up, and can't be found, eh? Never mind that," as Clarence laid Peyton's letter before him. "Can't read it now. Well, I suppose you want to be shipped back to Stockton?"

"No!" said the boy, recovering his voice with an effort.

"Eh, that's business, though. Know anybody here?"

"Not a living soul; that's why they sent me," said the boy, in sudden reckless desperation. He was the more furious that he knew the tears were standing in his eyes.

The idea seemed to strike the man amusingly. "Looks a little like it, don't it?" he said, smiling grimly at the paper before him. "Got any money?"

"A little."

"How much?"

"About twenty dollars," said Clarence hesitatingly. The man opened a drawer at his side, mechanically, for he did not raise his eyes, and took out two ten-dollar gold pieces. "I'll go twenty better," he said, laying them down on the desk. "That'll give you a chance to look around. Come back here, if you don't see your way clear." He dipped his pen into the ink with a significant gesture as if closing the interview.

Clarence pushed back the coin. "I'm not a beggar," he said doggedly.

The man this time raised his head and surveyed the boy with two keen eyes. "You're not, hey? Well, do I look like one?"

"No," stammered Clarence, as he glanced into the man's haughty eyes.

"Yet, if I were in your fix, I'd take that money and be glad to get it."

"If you'll let me pay you back again," said Clarence, a little ashamed, and considerably frightened at his implied accusation of the man before him.

"You can," said the man, bending over his desk again.

Clarence took up the money and awkwardly drew out his purse. But it was the first time he had touched it since it was returned to him in the bar-room, and it struck him that it was heavy and full—indeed, so full that on opening it a few coins rolled out on to the floor. The man looked up abruptly.

"I thought you said you had only twenty dollars?" he remarked grimly.

"Mr. Peyton gave me forty," returned Clarence, stupefied and blushing. "I spent twenty dollars for drinks at the bar—and," he stammered, "I—I—I don't know how the rest came here."

"You spent twenty dollars for ***drinks?***" said the man, laying down his pen, and leaning back, in his chair to gaze at the boy.

"Yes—that is—I treated some gentlemen of the stage, sir, at Davidson's Crossing.

"Did you treat the whole stage company?"

"No, sir, only about four or five—and the bar-keeper. But everything's so dear in California, *I* know that."

"Evidently. But it don't seem to make much difference with ***you,***" said the man, glancing at the purse.

"They wanted my purse to look at," said Clarence hurriedly, "and that's how the thing happened. Somebody put ***his own money*** back into ***my*** purse by accident."

"Of course," said the man grimly.

"Yes, that's the reason," said Clarence, a little relieved, but somewhat embarrassed by the man's persistent eyes.

"Then, of course," said the other quietly, "you don't require my twenty dollars now." "But," returned Clarence hesitatingly, "this isn't ***my*** money. I must find out who it belongs to, and give it back again. Perhaps," he added timidly, "I might leave it here with you, and call for it when I find the man, or send him here."

With the greatest gravity he here separated the surplus from what was left of Peyton's gift and the twenty dollars he had just received. The balance unaccounted, for was forty dollars. He laid it on the desk before the man, who, still looking at him, rose and opened the door.

"Mr. Reed."

The clerk who had shown Clarence in appeared.

"Open an account with"—He stopped and turned interrogatively to Clarence.

"Clarence Brant," said Clarence, coloring with excitement.

"With Clarence Brant. Take that deposit"—pointing to the money—"and give him a receipt." He paused as the clerk retired with a wondering gaze at the money, looked again at Clarence, said, "I think ***you'll*** do," and reëntered the private office, closing the door behind him.

I hope it will not be deemed inconceivable that Clarence, only a few moments before crushed with bitter disappointment and the hopeless revelation of his abandonment by his relatives, now felt himself lifted up suddenly into an imaginary height of independence and manhood. He was leaving the bank, in which he stood a minute before a friendless boy, not as a successful beggar, for this important man had disclaimed the idea, but absolutely as a customer! a depositor! a business man like the grown-up clients who were thronging the outer office, and before the eyes of the clerk who had pitied him! And he, Clarence, had been spoken to by this man, whose name he now recognized as the one that was on the door of the building—a man of whom his fellow-passengers had spoken with admiring envy—a banker famous in all California! Will it be deemed incredible that this imaginative and hopeful boy, forgetting all else, the object of his visit, and even the fact that he considered this money was not his own, actually put his hat a little on one side as he strolled out on his way to the streets and prospective fortune?

Two hours later the banker had another visitor. It chanced to be the farmer-looking man who had been Clarence's fellow-passenger. Evidently a privileged, person, he was at once ushered as "Captain Stevens" into the presence of the banker. At the end of a familiar business interview the captain asked carelessly— "Any letters for me?"

The busy banker pointed with his pen to the letter "S" in a row of alphabetically labeled pigeon-holes against the wall. The captain, having selected his correspondence, paused with a letter in his hand.

"Look here, Carden, there are letters here for some chap called 'John Silsbee.' They were here when I called, ten weeks ago."

"Well?"

"That's the name of that Pike County man who was killed by Injins in the plains. The 'Frisco papers had all the particulars last night; may be it's for that fellow. It hasn't got a postmark. Who left it here?"

Mr. Carden summoned a clerk. It appeared that the letter had been left by a certain Brant Fauquier, to be called for.

Captain Stevens smiled. "Brant's been too busy dealin' faro to think of 'em agin, and since that shootin' affair at Angels' I hear he's skipped to the southern coast somewhere. Cal Johnson, his old chum, was in the up stage from Stockton this afternoon."

"Did you come by the up stage from Stockton this afternoon?" said Carden, looking up.

"Yes, as far as Ten-mile Station—rode the rest of the way here."

"Did you notice a queer little old-fashioned kid—about so high—like a run-away school-boy?"

"Did I? By G—d, sir, he treated me to drinks."

Carden jumped from his chair. "Then he wasn't lying!"

"No! We let him do it; but we made it good for the little chap afterwards. Hello! What's up?"

But Mr. Carden was already in the outer office beside the clerk who had admitted Clarence.

"You remember that boy Brant who was here?"

"Yes, sir."

"Where did he go?"

"Don't know, sir."

"Go and find him somewhere and somehow. Go to all the hotels, restaurants, and gin-mills near here, and hunt him up. Take some one with you, if you can't do it alone. Bring him back here, quick!"

It was nearly midnight when the clerk fruitlessly returned. It was the fierce high noon of "steamer nights;" light flashed brilliantly from shops, counting-houses, drinking-saloons, and gambling-hells. The streets were yet full of eager, hurrying feet—swift to fortune, ambition, pleasure, or crime. But from among these deeper harsher foot-falls the echo of the homeless boy's light, innocent tread seemed to have died out forever.

CHAPTER VIII.

WHEN Clarence was once more in the busy street before the bank, it seemed clear to his boyish mind that, being now cast adrift upon the world, and responsible to no one, there was no reason why he should not at once proceed to the nearest gold mines! The idea of returning to Mr. Peyton and Susy, as a disowned and abandoned outcast, was not to be thought of. He would purchase some kind of an outfit, such as he had seen the miners carry, and start off as soon as he had got his supper. But although one of his most delightful anticipations had been the unfettered freedom of ordering a meal at a restaurant, on entering the first one he found himself the object of so much curiosity, partly from his size and partly from his dress, which the unfortunate boy was beginning to suspect was really preposterous, that he turned away with, a stammered, excuse, and did not try another. Further on he found a baker's shop, where he refreshed himself with some gingerbread and lemon soda. At an adjacent grocery he purchased some herrings, smoked beef, and biscuits, as future provisions for his "pack" or kit. Then began his real quest for an outfit. In an hour he had secured—ostensibly for some friend, to avoid curious inquiry—pan, a blanket, a shovel and pick, all of which he deposited at the baker's, his unostentatious headquarters, with the exception of a pair of disguising high boots that half hid his sailor trousers, which he kept to put on at the last. Even to his inexperience the cost of these articles seemed enormous; when his purchases were complete, of his entire capital scarcely four dollars remained! Yet in the fond illusions of boyhood these rude appointments seemed possessed of far more value than the gold he had given in exchange for them, and he had enjoyed a child's delight in testing the transforming magic of money. Meanwhile, the feverish contact of the crowded street had, strange to say, increased his loneliness, while the ruder joviality of its dissipations began to fill him with a vague uneasiness. The passing glimpse of dancing halls and gaudily whirling figures that seemed only feminine in their apparel; the shouts and boisterous choruses from concert rooms; the groups of drunken roisterers that congregated around the doors of saloons or, hilariously charging down the streets, elbowed him against the wall, or humorously insisted on his company, discomposed and frightened him. He had known rude companionship before, but it was serious, practical, and under control. There was something in this vulgar degradation of intellect and power—qualities that Clarence had always boyishly worshiped—which sickened and disillusioned him. Later on a pistol shot in a crowd beyond, the rush of eager men past him, the disclosure of a limp and helpless figure against the wall, the closing of the crowd again around it, although it stirred him with a fearful curiosity, actually shocked him less hopelessly than their brutish enjoyments and abandonment.

It was in one of these rushes that he had been crushed against a swinging door, which, giving way to his pressure, disclosed to his wondering eyes a long, glitteringly adorned, and brightly lit room, densely filled with a silent, attentive throng in attitudes of decorous abstraction and preoccupation, that even the shouts and tumult at its very doors could not disturb. Men of all ranks and conditions, plainly or elaborately clad, were grouped together under this magic spell of silence and attention. The tables before them were covered with cards and loose heaps of gold and silver. A clicking, the rattling of an ivory ball, and the frequent, formal, lazy reiteration of some unintelligible sentence was all that he heard. But by a sudden instinct he **understood** it all. It was a gambling saloon!

Encouraged by the decorous stillness, and the fact that everybody appeared too much engaged to notice him, the boy drew timidly beside one of the tables. It was covered with a number of cards, on which were placed certain sums of money. Looking down, Clarence saw that he was standing before a card that as yet had nothing on it. A single player at his side looked up, glanced at Clarence curiously, and then placed half a dozen gold pieces on the vacant card. Absorbed in the general aspect of the room and the players, Clarence did not notice that his neighbor won twice, and even **thrice,** upon that card. Becoming aware, however, that the player, while gathering in his gains, was smilingly regarding him he moved in some embarrassment to the other end of the table, where there seemed another gap in the crowd. It so chanced that here was also another vacant card. The previous neighbor of Clarence instantly shoved a sum of money across the table on the vacant card and won! At this the other players began to regard Clarence singularly, one or two of the spectators smiled, and the boy, coloring, moved awkwardly away. But his sleeve was caught by the successful player, who, detaining him gently, put three gold pieces into his hand.

"That's **your** share, sonny," he whispered.

"Share—for what?" stammered the astounded Clarence.

"For bringing me 'the luck,'" said the man.

Clarence stared. "Am I—to—to play with it?" he said, glancing at the coins and then at the table, in ignorance of the stranger's meaning.

"No, no!" said the man hurriedly, "don't do that. You'll lose it, sonny, sure! Don't you see, **you bring the luck to others,** not to yourself. Keep it, old man, and run home!"

"I don't want it! I won't have it!" said Clarence, with a swift recollection of the manipulation of his purse that morning, and a sudden distrust of all mankind.

"There!" He turned back to the table and laid the money on the first vacant card he saw. In another moment, as it seemed to him, it was raked away by the dealer. A sense of relief came over him.

"There!" said the man, with an awed voice and a strange, fatuous look in his eye. "What did I tell you? You see, it's allus so! Now," he added roughly, "get up and get out o' this, afore you lose the boots and shirt off ye."

Clarence did not wait for a second command. With another glance round the room, he began to make his way through the crowd towards the front. But in that parting glance lie caught a glimpse of a woman presiding over a "wheel of fortune" in a corner, whose face seemed familiar. He looked again, timidly. In spite of an extraordinary head-dress or crown that she wore as the "Goddess of Fortune," he recognized, twisted in its tinsel, a certain scarlet vine which he had seen before; in spite of the hoarse formula which she was continually repeating, he recognized the foreign accent. It was the woman of the stagecoach! With a sudden dread that she might recognize him, and likewise demand his services "for luck," he turned and fled.

Once more in the open air, there came upon him a vague loathing and horror of the restless madness and feverish distraction of this half-civilized city. It was the more powerful that it was vague, and the outcome of some inward instinct. He found himself longing for the pure air and sympathetic loneliness of the plains and wilderness; he began to yearn for the companionship of his humble associates—the teamster, the scout Gildersleeve, and even Jim Hooker. But above all and before all was the wild desire to get away from these maddening streets and their bewildering occupants. He ran back to the baker's, gathered his purchases together, took advantage of a friendly doorway to strap them on his boyish shoulders, slipped into a side street, and struck out at once for the outskirts.

It had been his first intention to take stage to the nearest mining district, but the diminution of his small capital forbade that outlay, and he decided to walk there by the highroad, of whose general direction he had informed himself. In half an hour the lights of the flat, struggling city, and their reflection in the shallow, turbid river before it, had sunk well behind him. The air was cool and soft; a yellow moon swam in the slight haze that rose above the *tules;* in the distance a few scattered cottonwoods and sycamores marked like sentinels the road. When he had walked some distance he sat down beneath one of them to make a frugal supper from the dry rations in his pack, but in the absence of any spring he was forced to quench his thirst with a glass of water in a wayside tavern. Here he was good-humoredly offered something stronger, which he declined, and replied to certain curious interrogations by saying mat he expected to overtake his friends in a wagon further on. A new distrust of mankind had begun to make the boy an adept in innocent falsehood, the more deceptive as his careless, cheerful manner, the result of his relief at leaving the city, and his perfect ease in the loving companionship of night and nature, certainly gave no indication of his homelessness and poverty.

It was long past midnight when, weary in body, but still hopeful and happy in mind, he turned oil the dusty road into a vast rolling expanse of wild oats, with the same sense of security of rest as a traveler to his inn. Here, completely screened from view by the tall stalks of grain that rose thickly around him to the height of a man's shoulder, he beat down a few of them for a bed, on which he deposited his blanket. Placing his pack for a pillow, he curled himself up in his blanket, and speedily fell asleep.

He awoke at sunrise, refreshed, invigorated, and hungry. But he was forced to defer his first self-prepared breakfast until he had reached water, and a less dangerous place than the wild-oat field to build his first camp fire. This he found a mile further on, near some dwarf willows on the bank of a half-dry stream. Of his various efforts to prepare his first meal, the fire was the most successful; the coffee was somewhat too substantially thick, and the bacon and herring lacked definiteness of quality from having been cooked in the same vessel. In this boyish picnic he missed Susy, and recalled, perhaps a little bitterly, her coldness at parting. But the novelty of his situation, the brilliant sunshine and sense of freedom, and the road already awakening to dusty life with passing teams, dismissed everything but the future from his mind. Readjusting his pack, he stepped on cheerily. At noon he was overtaken by a teamster, who in return for a match to light his pipe gave him a lift of a dozen miles. It is to be feared that Clarence's account of himself was equally fanciful with his previous story, and that the teamster parted from him with a genuine regret, and a hope that he would soon be overtaken by his friends along the road. "And mind that you ain't such a fool agin to let 'em make you tote their dod-blasted tools fur them!" he added unsuspectingly, pointing to Clarence's mining outfit. Thus saved the heaviest part of the day's journey, for the road was continually rising from the plains during the last six miles, Clarence was able yet to cover a considerable distance on foot before he halted for supper. Here he was again fortunate. An empty lumber team watering at the same spring, its driver offered, to take Clarence's purchases—for the boy had profited by his late friend's suggestion to personally detach himself from his equipment—to Buckeye Mills for a dollar, which would also include a "shakedown passage" for himself on the floor of the wagon. "I reckon you've been foolin' away in Sacramento the money yer parents give yer fur return stage fare, eh? Don't lie, sonny," he added grimly, as the now artful Clarence smiled diplomatically. "I've been that myself!" Luckily, the excuse that he was "tired and sleepy" prevented further dangerous questioning, and the boy was soon really in deep slumber on the wagon floor.

He awoke betimes to find himself already in the mountains. Buckeye Mills was a straggling settlement, and Clarence prudently stopped any embarrassing inquiry from his friend by dropping off the wagon with his equipment as they entered it, and hurriedly saying "Good-by" from a crossroad, through the woods. He had learned that the nearest mining camp was five miles away, and its direction was indicated by a long wooden "flume," or water-way, that alternately appeared and disappeared on me flank of the mountain opposite. The cooler and drier air, the grateful shadow of pine and bay, and the spicy balsamic odors that everywhere greeted him thrilled and exhilarated him. The trail plunging sometimes into an undisturbed forest, he started the birds before him like a flight of arrows through its dim recesses; at times he hung breathlessly over the blue depths of cañons where the same forests were repeated a thousand feet below. Towards noon he struck into a rude road—evidently the thoroughfare of the locality—and was surprised to find that it, as well as the adjacent soil wherever disturbed, was a deep Indian red. Everywhere, along its sides, powdering the banks and boles of trees with its ruddy stain, in mounds and hillocks of piled dirt on the road, or in liquid paint-like pools, when a trickling stream had formed a gutter across it, there was always the same deep sanguinary color. Once or twice it became more vivid, in contrast with, the white teeth of quartz that peeped through it from the hillside or crossed the road in crumbled strata. One of those pieces Clarence picked up with a quickened pulse. It was veined and streaked with sliming mica and tiny glittering cubes of mineral that ***looked*** like gold!

The road now began to descend towards a winding stream, shrunken by drought and ditching, that glared dazzlingly in the sunlight from its white bars of sand, or glistened in shining sheets and channels. Along its banks, and even encroaching upon its bed, were scattered a few mud cabins, strange-looking wooden troughs and gutters, and here and there, glancing through the leaves, the white canvas of tents. The stumps of felled trees and blackened spaces, as of recent fires, marked the stream on either side. A sudden sense of disappointment overcame Clarence. It looked vulgar, common, and worse than all—*familiar.* It was like the unlovely outskirts of a dozen other prosaic settlements he had seen in less romantic localities. In that muddy red stream, pouring out of a wooden gutter, in which three or four bearded, slouching, half-naked figures were raking like ***chiffonniers,*** there was nothing to suggest the royal metal. Yet he was so absorbed in gazing at the scene, and had walked so rapidly during the past few minutes, that he was startled, on turning a sharp corner of the road, to come abruptly upon an outlying dwelling.

It was a nondescript building, half canvas and half boards. The interior seen through the open door was fitted up with side shelves, a counter carelessly piled with provisions, groceries, clothing, and hardware—with no attempt at display or even ordinary selection—and a table, on which stood a demijohn and three or four dirty glasses. Two roughly dressed men, whose long, matted beards and hair left only their eyes and lips visible in the tangled hirsute wilderness below their slouched hats, were leaning against the opposite sides of the doorway, smoking. Almost thrown against them in the rapid momentum of his descent, Clarence halted violently.

"Well, sonny, you needn't capsize the shanty," said the first man, without taking his pipe from his lips.

"If yer looking fur yer ma, she and yer Aunt Jane hev jest gone over to Parson Doolittle's to take tea," observed the second man lazily. "She allowed that you'd wait."

"I'm—I'm—going to—to the mines," explained Clarence, with some hesitation. "I suppose this is the way."

The two men took their pipes from their lips, looked at each other, completely wiped every vestige of expression from their faces with the back of their hands, turned their eyes into the interior of the cabin, and said, "Will yer come yer, now *will* yer?" Thus adjured, half a dozen men, also bearded find carrying pipes in their mouths, straggled out of the shanty, and, filing in front of it, squatted down, with their backs against the boards, and gazed comfortably at the boy. Clarence began to feel uneasy.

"I'll give," said one, taking out his pipe and grimly eying Clarence, "a hundred dollars for him as he stands."

"And seein' as he's got that bran-new rig-out o' tools," said another, "I'll give a hundred and fifty—and the drinks. I've been," he added apologetically, "wantin' suthin' like this a long time."

"Well, gen'lemen," said the man who had first spoken to him, "lookin' at him by and large; takin' in, so to speak, the gin'ral gait of him in single harness; bearin' in mind, the perfect freshness of him, and the coolness and size of his cheek—the easy downyness, previousness, and utter don't care-a-damnativeness of his coining yer, I think two hundred ain't too much for him, and we'll call it a bargain."

Clarence's previous experience of this grim, smileless Californian chaff was not calculated to restore his confidence. He drew away from the cabin, and repeated doggedly, "I asked you if this was the way to the mines."

"It *are* the mines, and these yere are the miners," said the first speaker gravely. "Permit me to interdoose 'em. This yere's Shasta Jim, this yere's Shortcard Billy, this is Nasty Bob, and this Slumgullion Dick. This yere's the Dook o' Chatham Street, the Livin' Skeleton, and me!"

"May we ask, fair young sir," said the Living Skeleton, who, however, seemed in fairly robust condition, "whence came ye on the wings of the morning, and whose Marble Halls ye hev left desolate?"

"I came across the plains, and got into Stockton two days ago on Mr. Peyton's train," said Clarence, indignantly, seeing no reason now to conceal anything. "I came to Sacramento to find, my cousin, who isn't living there any more. I don't see anything funny in *that!* I came here to the mines to dig gold—because—because Mr. Silsbee, the man who was to bring me here and might have found my cousin for me, was killed by Indians."

"Hold up, sonny. Let me help ye," said the first speaker, rising to his feet. "***You*** didn't get killed by Injins because you got lost out of a train with Silsbee's infant darter. Peyton picked you up while you was takin' care of her, and two days arter you kem up to the broken-down Silsbee wagons, with all the folks lyin' there slar-tered." "Yes, sir," said Clarence, breathless with astonishment.

"And," continued the man, putting his, hand gravely to his head as if to as-sist his memory, "when you was all alone on the plains with that little child you saw one of those redskins, as near to you as I be, watchin' the train, and you didn't breathe or move while he was there?"

"Yes, sir," said Clarence eagerly.

"And you was shot at by Peyton, he thinkin' you was an Injin in the mesquite grass? And you once shot a buffalo that had been pitched with you down a gully— all by yourself?"

"Yes," said Clarence, crimson with wonder and pleasure. "You know me, then?"

"Well, ye-e-es," said the man gravely, parting his mustache with his fingers. "You see, *you've been here before.*"

"Before! Me?" repeated the astounded Clarence.

"Yes, before. Last night. You was taller then, and hadn't cut your hair. You cursed a good deal more than you do now. You drank a man's share of whiskey, and you borrowed fifty dollars to get to Sacramento with. I reckon you haven't got it about you now, eh?"

Clarence's brain reeled in utter confusion and hopeless terror.

Was he going crazy, or had these cruel men learned his story from his faith-less friends, and this was a part of the plot? He staggered forward, but the men had risen and quickly encircled him, as if to prevent his escape. In vague and helpless desperation he gasped—

"What place is this?"

"Folks call it Deadman's Gulch."

Deadman's Gulch! A flash of intelligence lit up the boy's blind confusion. Dead-man's Gulch! Could it have been Jim Hooker who had really run away, and had taken his name? He turned half imploringly to the first speaker.

"Wasn't he older than me, and bigger? Didn't he have a smooth, round face and little eyes? Didn't he talk hoarse? Didn't he"—He stopped hopelessly. "Yes; oh, he wasn't a bit like you," said the man musingly. "Ye see, that's the h-ll of it! You're altogether *too many* and *too various* fur this camp."

"I don't know who's been here before, or what they have said, said Clarence desperately, yet even in that desperation retaining the dogged loyalty to his old playmate which was part of his nature. "I don't know, and I don't care—there! I'm Clarence Brant, of Kentucky; I started in Silsbee's train from St. Jo, and I'm going to the mines, and you can't stop me!"

The man who had first spoken started, looked keenly at Clarence, and then turned to the others. The gentleman known as the Living Skeleton had obtruded his huge bulk in front of the boy, and, gazing at him, said reflectively, "Darned if it don't look like one of Brant's pups—sure!"

"Air ye any relation to Kernel Hamilton Brant, of Looeyville?" asked the first speaker.

Again that old question! Poor Clarence hesitated, despairingly. Was he to go through the same cross-examination he had undergone with the Peytons? "Yes," he said doggedly, "I am—but he's dead, and you know it."

"Dead—of course." "Sartin." "He's dead." "The Kernel's planted, said the men in chorus.

"Well yes," reflected the Living Skeleton ostentatiously, as one who spoke from experience. "Ham Brant's about as bony now as they make 'em."

"You bet! About the dustiest, deadest corpse you kin turn out," corroborated Slumgullion Dick, nodding his head gloomily to the others; "in point o' fack, es a corpse, about the last one I should keer to go huntin' fur."

"The Kernel's tech 'ud be cold and clammy," concluded the Duke of Chatham Street, who had not yet spoken, "sure. But what did yer mammy say about it? Is she gettin' married agin? Did *she* send ye here?"

It seemed to Clarence that the Duke of Chatham Street here received a kick from his companions; due the boy repeated doggedly—

"I came to Sacramento to find my cousin, Jackson Brant; but he wasn't there."

"Jackson Brant!" echoed the first speaker, glancing at the others. "Did your mother say he was your cousin?"

"Yes," said Clarence wearily. "Good-by."

"Hullo, sonny, where are you going?"

"To dig gold," said the boy. "And you know you can't prevent me, if it isn't on your claim. I know the law." He had heard Mr. Peyton discuss it at Stockton, and he fancied that the men, who were whispering among themselves, looked kinder than before, and as if they were no longer "acting" to him. The first speaker laid, his hand on his shoulder, and said, "All right, come with me, and I'll show you where to dig."

"Who are you?" said Clarence. "You called yourself only 'me.'"

"Well, you can call me Flynn—Tom Flynn."

"And you'll show me where I can dig—myself?"

"I will."

"Do you know," said Clarence timidly, yet with a half-conscious smile, "that I—I kinder bring luck?"

The man looked down upon him, and said gravely, but, as it struck Clarence, with a new kind of gravity, "I believe you."

"Yes," said Clarence eagerly, as they walked along together, "I brought luck to a man in Sacramento the other clay." And he related with great earnestness his experience in the gambling saloon. Not content with that—the sealed fountains of his childish deep being broken up by some mysterious sympathy—he spoke of his hospitable exploit with the passengers at the wayside bar, of the finding of his Fortunatus purse and his deposit at the bank. Whether that characteristic old-fashioned reticence which had been such an important factor for good or ill in his future had suddenly deserted him, or whether some extraordinary prepossession in his companion had affected him, he did not know; but by the time the pair had reached the hillside Flynn was in possession of all the boy's history. On one point only was his reserve unshaken. Conscious although he was of Jim Hooker's duplicity, he affected to treat it as a comrade's joke.

They halted at last in the middle of an apparently fertile hillside. Clarence shifted his shovel from his shoulders, unslung his pan, and looked at Flynn. "Dig anywhere here, where you like," said his companion carelessly, "and you'll be sure to find the color. Fill your pan with the dirt, go to that sluice, and let the water run in on the top of the pan—workin' it round so," he added, illustrating a rotary motion with the vessel. "Keep doing that until all the soil is washed out of it, and you have only the black sand, at the bottom. Then work that the same way until you see the color. Don't be afraid of washing the gold out of the pan—you couldn't do it if you tried. There, I'll leave you here, and you wait till I come back." With another grave nod and something like a smile in the only visible part of his bearded face—his eyes—he strode rapidly away.

Clarence did not lose time. Selecting a spot where the grass was less thick, he broke through the soil and turned up two or three spadefuls of red soil. When he had filled the pan and raised it to his shoulder, he was astounded at its weight. He did not know that it was due to the red precipitate of iron that gave it its color. Staggering along with his burden to the running sluice, which looked like an open wooden gutter, at the foot of the hill, he began to carefully carry out Flynn's direction. The first dip of the pan in the running water carried off half the contents of the pan in liquid paint-like ooze. For a moment he gave way to boyish satisfaction in the sight and touch of this unctuous solution, and dabbled his fingers in it. A few moments more of rinsing and he came to the sediment of fine black sand that was beneath it. Another plunge and swilling of water in the pan, and—could he believe his eyes!—a few yellow tiny scales, scarcely larger than pins' heads, glittered among the sand. He poured it off. But his companion was right; the lighter sand shifted from side to side with the water, but the glittering points remained adhering by their own tiny specific gravity to the smooth surface of the bottom. It was "the color"—gold!

Clarence's heart seemed to give a great leap within him. A vision of wealth, of independence, of power, sprang before his dazzled eyes, and—a hand lightly touched him on the shoulder.

He started. In his complete preoccupation and excitement, he had not heard the clatter of horse-hoofs, and to his amazement Flynn was already beside him, mounted, and leading a second horse.

"You kin ride?" he said shortly.

"Yes," stammered Clarence; "but"—

"***But***—we've only got two hours to reach Buckeye Mills in time to catch the down stage. Drop all that, jump up, and come with me!"

"But I've just found gold," said the boy excitedly.

"And I've just found your—cousin. Come!"

He spurred his horse across Clarence's scattered implements, half helped, half lifted, the boy into the saddle of the second horse, and, with a cut of his riata over the animal's haunches, the next moment they were both galloping furiously away.

CHAPTER IX.

TORN suddenly from his prospective future, but too much dominated by the man beside him to protest, Clarence was silent until a rise in the road, a few minutes later, partly abated their headlong speed, and gave him chance to recover his breath and courage.

"Where is my cousin?" he asked.

"In the Southern county, two hundred miles from here."

"Are we going to him?"

"Yes."

They rode furiously forward again. It was nearly half an hour before they came to a longer ascent. Clarence could see that Flynn was from time to time examining him curiously under his slouched hat. This somewhat embarrassed him, but in his singular confidence in the man no distrust mingled with it.

"Ye never saw your—cousin?" he asked.

"No," said Clarence; "nor he me. I don't think he knew me much, any way."

"How old mout ye be, Clarence?"

"Eleven."

"Well, as you're suthin of a pup"—Clarence started, and recalled Peyton's first criticism of him—"I reckon to tell ye suthin. Ye ain't goin' to be skeert, or afeard, or lose yer sand, I kalkilate, for skunkin' ain't in your breed. Well, wot ef I told ye that thish yer—thish yer—*cousin* o' yours was the biggest devil onhung; that he'd just killed a man, and had to lite out elsewhere, and *thet's* why he didn't show up in Sacramento—what if I told you that?"

Clarence felt that this was somehow a little too much. He was perfectly truthful, and lifting his frank eyes to Flynn, he said, "I should think you were talking a good deal like Jim Hooker!" His companion stared, and suddenly reined up his horse; then, bursting into a shout of laughter, he galloped ahead, from time to time shaking his head, slapping his legs, and making the dim woods ring with his boisterous mirth. Then as suddenly becoming thoughtful again, he rode on rapidly for half an hour, only speaking to Clarence to urge him forward, and assisting his progress by lashing the haunches of his horse. Luckily, the boy was a good rider—a fact which Flynn seemed to thoroughly appreciate—or he would have been unseated a dozen times.

At last the straggling sheds of Buckeye Mills came into softer purple view on the opposite mountain. Then laying his hand on Clarence's shoulder as he reined in at his side, Flynn broke the silence.

"There, boy," he said, wiping the mirthful tears from his eyes. "I was only foolin'—only tryin' yer grit! This yer cousin I'm taking you to ez as quiet and soft-spoken and as old-fashioned ez you be. Why, he's that wrapped up in books and study that he lives alone in a big *adobe rancherie* among a lot o' Spanish, and he don't keer to see his own countrymen! Why, he's even changed his name, and calls himself Don Juan Robinson! But he's very rich; he owns three leagues of land and heaps of cattle and horses, and," glancing approvingly at Clarence's seat in the saddle, "I reckon you'll hev plenty of fun thar."

"But," hesitated Clarence, to whom this proposal seemed only a repetition of Peyton's charitable offer, "I think I'd better stay here and dig gold—*with you.*"

"And I think you'd better not," said the man, with a gravity that was very like a settled determination.

"But my cousin never came for me to Sacramento—nor sent, nor even wrote," persisted Clarence indignantly.

"Not to *you,* boy; but he wrote to the man whom he reckoned would bring you there—Jack Silsbee—and left it in the care of the bank. And Silsbee, being dead, didn't come for the letter; and as you didn't ask for it when you came, and didn't even mention Silsbee's name, that same letter was sent back to your cousin through me, because the bank thought we knew his whereabouts. It came to the gulch by an express rider, whilst you were prospectin' on the hillside. Rememberin' your story, I took the liberty of opening it, and found out that your cousin had told Silsbee to bring you straight to him. So I'm only doin' now what Silsbee would have done."

Any momentary doubt or suspicion that might have risen in Clarence's mind vanished as he met his companion's steady and masterful eye. Even his disappointment was forgotten in the charm of this new-found friendship and protection. And as its outset had been marked by an unusual burst of confidence on Clarence's part, the boy, in his gratitude, now felt something of the timid shyness of a deeper feeling, and once more became reticent.

They were in time to snatch a hasty meal at Buckeye Mills before the stage and Clarence noticed that his friend, despite his rough dress and lawless aspect, provoked a marked degree of respect from those he met—in which, perhaps, a wholesome fear was mingled. It is certain that the two best places in the stage were given up to them without protest, and that a careless, almost supercilious invitation to drink from Flynn was responded to with singular alacrity by all, including even two fastidiously dressed and previously reserved passengers. I am afraid that Clarence enjoyed this proof of his friend's singular dominance with a boyish pride, and, conscious of the curious eyes of the passengers, directed occasionally to himself, was somewhat ostentatious in his familiarity with this bearded autocrat.

At noon the next day they left the stage at a wayside road station, and Flynn briefly informed Clarence that they must again take horses. This at first seemed difficult in mat out-of-the-way settlement, where they alone had stopped, but a whisper from the driver in the ear of the station-master produced a couple of fiery mustangs, with the same accompaniment of cautious awe and mystery. For the next two days they traveled on horseback, resting by night at the lodgings of one or other of Flynn's friends in the outskirts of a large town, where they arrived in the darkness, and left before day. To any one more experienced than the simple-minded boy it would have been evident that Flynn was purposely avoiding the more traveled roads and conveyances; and when they changed horses again the next day's ride was through an apparently unbroken wilderness of scattered wood and rolling plain. Yet to Clarence, with his pantheistic reliance and joyous sympathy with nature, the change was filled with exhilarating pleasure. The vast seas of tossing wild oats, the hillside still variegated with strange flowers, the virgin freshness of untrodden woods and leafy aisles, whose floors of moss or bark were undisturbed by human footprint, were a keen delight and novelty. More than this, his quick eye, trained perceptions, and frontier knowledge now stood him in good stead. His intuitive sense of distance, instincts of wood-craft, and his unerring detection of those signs, landmarks, and guide-posts of nature, undistinguishable to aught but birds and beasts and some children, were now of the greatest service to his less favored companion. In this part of their strange pilgrimage it was the boy who took the lead. Flynn, who during the past two days seemed to have fallen into a mood of watchful reserve, nodded his approbation. "This sort of thing's yer best holt, boy," he said. "Men and cities ain't your little game." At the next stopping-place Clarence had a surprise. They had again entered a town at nightfall, and lodged with another friend of Flynn's in rooms which from vague sounds appeared to be over a gambling saloon. Clarence woke late in the morning, and, descending into the street to mount for the day's journey, was startled to find that Flynn was not on the other horse, but that a well-dressed and handsome stranger had taken his place. But a laugh, and the familiar command, "Jump up, boy," made him look again. It *was* Flynn, but completely shaven of beard and mustache, closely clipped of hair, and in a fastidiously cut suit of black!

"Then you didn't know me?" said Flynn.

"Not till you spoke," replied Clarence.

"So much the better," said his friend sententiously, as he put spurs to his horse. But as they cantered through the street, Clarence, who had already become accustomed to the stranger's hirsute adornment, felt a little more awe of him. The profile of the mouth and chin now exposed to his sidelong glance was hard and stern, and slightly saturnine. Although unable at the time to identify it with anybody he had ever known, it seemed to the imaginative boy to be vaguely connected with some sad experience. But the eyes were thoughtful and kindly, and the boy later believed that if he had been more familiar with the face he would have loved it better. For it was the last and only day he was to see it, as, late that afternoon, after a dusty ride along more traveled highways, they reached their journey's end.

It was a low-walled house, with red-tiled roofs showing against the dark green of venerable pear and fig trees, and a square courtyard in the centre, where they had dismounted. A few words in Spanish from Flynn to one of the lounging peons admitted them to a wooden corridor, and thence to a long, low room, which to Clarence's eyes seemed literally piled with books and engravings. Here Flynn hurriedly bade him stay while he sought the host in another part of the building. But Clarence did not miss him; indeed, it may be feared, he forgot even the object of their journey in the new sensations that suddenly thronged upon him, and the boyish vista of the future that they seemed to open. He was dazed and intoxicated. He had never seen so many books before; he had never conceived of such lovely pictures. And yet in some vague way he thought he must have dreamt of them at some time. He had mounted a chair, and was gazing spellbound at an engraving of a sea-fight, when he heard Flynn's voice.

His friend had quietly reëntered the room, company with an oldish, half-foreign-looking man, evidently his relation. With no helping recollection, with no means of comparison beyond a vague idea that his cousin might look like himself, Clarence stood hopelessly before him. He had already made up his mind that he would have to go through the usual cross-questioning in regard to his father and family; he had even forlornly thought of inventing some innocent details to fill out his imperfect and unsatisfactory recollection. But, glancing up, he was surprised to find that his elderly cousin was as embarrassed as he was. Flynn, as usual, masterfully interposed.

"Of course ye don't remember each other, and thar ain't much that either of you knows about family matters, I reckon," he said grimly; "and as your cousin calls himself Don Juan Robinson," he added to Clarence, "it's just as well that you let 'Jackson Brant' slide. I know him better than you, but you'll get used to him, and he to you, soon enough. At least, you'd better," he concluded, with his singular gravity.

As he turned as if to leave the room with Clarence's embarrassed relative—much to that gentleman's apparent relief—the boy looked up at the latter and said timidly—

"May I look at those books?"

His cousin stopped, and glanced at him with the first expression of interest he had shown.

"Ah, you read; you like books?"

"Yes," said Clarence. As his cousin remained still looking at him thoughtfully, he added, "My hands are pretty clean, but I can wash them first, if you like."

"You may look at them," said Don Juan smilingly; "and as they are old books you can wash your hands afterwards." And, turning to Flynn suddenly, with an air of relief, I tell you what I'll do—I'll teach him Spanish!"

They left the room together, and Clarence turned eagerly to the shelves. They were old books, some indeed very old, queerly bound, and worm-eaten. Some were in foreign languages, but others in clear, bold English type, with quaint wood-cuts and illustrations. One seemed to be a chronicle of battles and sieges, with pictured representations of combatants spitted with arrows, cleanly lopped off in limb, or toppled over distinctly by visible cannon-shot. He was deep in its perusal when he heard the clatter of horse's hoofs in the court-yard and the voice of Flynn. He ran to the window, and was astonished to see his friend already on horseback, taking leave of his host.

For one instant Clarence felt one of those sudden revulsions of feeling common to his age, but which he had always timidly hidden under dogged demeanor. Flynn, his only friend! Flynn, his only boyish confidant! Flynn, his latest hero, was going away and forsaking him without a word of parting! It was true that he had only agreed to take him to his guardian, but still Flynn need not have left him without a word of hope or encouragement! With any one else Clarence would probably have taken refuge in his usual Indian stoicism, but the same feeling that had impelled him to offer Flynn his boyish confidences on their first meeting now overpowered him. He dropped his book, ran out into the corridor, and made his way to the court-yard, just as Flynn galloped out from the arch.

But the boy uttered a despairing shout that reached the rider. He drew rein, wheeled, halted, and sat facing Clarence impatiently. To add to Clarence's embarrassment his cousin had lingered in the corridor, attracted by the interruption, and a peon, lounging in the archway, obsequiously approached Flynn's bridle-rein. But the rider waved him off, and, turning sternly to Clarence, said:—

"What's the matter now?"

"Nothing," said Clarence, striving to keep back the hot tears that rose in his eyes. "But you were going away without saying 'good-by.' You've been very kind to me, and—and—I want to thank you!"

A deep flush crossed Flynn's face. Then glancing suspiciously towards the corridor, he said hurriedly,—

"Did *he* send you?"

"No, I came myself. I heard you going."

"All right. Good-by." He leaned forward, as if about to take Clarence's out stretched hand, checked himself suddenly with a grim smile, and taking from his pocket a gold coin handed it to the boy.

Clarence took it, tossed it with a proud gesture to the waiting peon, who caught it thankfully, drew back a step from Flynn, and saying, with white cheeks, "I only wanted to say good-by," dropped his hot eyes to the ground. But it did not seem to be his own voice that had spoken, nor his own self that had prompted the act.

There was a quick interchange of glances between the departing guest and his late host, in which Flynn's eyes flashed with an odd, admiring fire, but when Clarence raised his head again he was gone. And as the boy turned back with a broken heart towards the corridor, his cousin laid his hand upon his shoulder.

"***Muy hidalgamente,*** Clarence, he said pleasantly. "Yes, we shall make something of you!"

CHAPTER X.

THEN followed to Clarence three uneventful years. During that interval he learnt that Jackson Brant, or Don Juan Robinson—for the tie of kinship was the least factor in their relations to each other, and after the departure of Flynn was tacitly ignored by both—was more Spanish than American. An early residence in Lower California, marriage with a rich Mexican widow, whose dying childless left him sole heir, and   some strange restraining idiosyncrasy of temperament had quite denationalized him. A bookish recluse, somewhat superfastidious towards his own countrymen, the more Clarence knew him the more singular appeared his acquaintance with Flynn; but as he did not exhibit more communicativeness on this point than upon their own kinship, Clarence finally concluded that it was due to the dominant character of his former friend, and thought no more about it. He entered upon the new life at El Refugio with no disturbing past. Quickly adapting himself to the lazy freedom of this ***hacienda*** existence, he spent the mornings on horseback ranging the hills among his cousin's cattle, and the afternoons and evenings busied among his cousin's books with equally lawless and undisciplined independence. The easy- going Don Juan, it is true, attempted to make good his rash promise to teach the boy Spanish, and actually set him a few tasks; but in a few weeks the quick-witted Clarence acquired such a colloquial proficiency from his casual acquaintance with vaqueros and small traders that he was glad to leave the matter in his young kinsman's hands. Again, by one of those illogical sequences which make a lifelong reputation depend upon a single trivial act, Clarence's social status was settled forever at El Refugio Rancho by his picturesque diversion of Flynn's parting gift. The grateful peon to whom the boy had scornfully tossed the coin repeated the act, gesture, and spirit of the scene to his companion, and Don Juan's unknown and youthful relation was at once recognized as *hijo de la familia,* and undeniably a hidalgo born and bred. But in the more vivid imagination of feminine El Refugio the incident reached its highest poetic form. "It is true, Mother of God," said Chucha of the Mill; "it was Domingo who himself relates it as it were the Creed. When the American escort has arrived with the young gentleman, this escort, look you, being not of the same quality, he is departing again without a word of permission. Comes to him at this moment my little hidalgo. 'You have yourself forgotten to take from me your demission,' he said. This escort, thinking to make his peace with a mere *muchacho,* gives to him a gold piece of twenty pesos. The little hidalgo has taken it *so,* and with the words, ' Ah! you would make of me your almoner to my cousin's people,' has given it at the moment to Domingo, and with a grace and fire admirable." But it is certain that Clarence's singular simplicity and truthfulness, a faculty of being picturesquely indolent in a way that suggested a dreamy abstraction of mind rather than any vulgar tendency to bodily ease and comfort, and possibly the fact that he was a good horseman, made him a popular hero at El Refugio. At the end of three years Don Juan found that this inexperienced and apparently idle boy of fourteen knew more of the practical ruling of the ranche than he did himself; also that this unlettered young rustic had devoured nearly all the books in his library with boyish recklessness of digestion. He found, too, that in spite of his singular independence of action, Clarence was possessed of an invincible loyalty of principle, and that, asking no sentimental affection, and indeed yielding none, he was, without presuming on his relationship, devoted to his cousin's interest. It seemed that from being a glancing ray of sunshine in the house, evasive but never obtrusive, he had become a daily necessity of comfort and security to his benefactor.

Clarence was, however, astonished, when, one morning, Don Juan, with the same embarrassed manner he had shown at their first meeting, suddenly asked him, "what business he expected, to follow." It seemed the more singular, as the speaker, like most abstracted, men, had hitherto always studiously ignored the future, in their daily intercourse. Yet this might have been either the habit of security or the caution of doubt. Whatever it was, it was some sudden disturbance of Don Juan's equanimity, as disconcerting to himself as it was to Clarence. So conscious was the boy of this that, without replying to his cousin's question, but striving in vain to recall some delinquency of his own, he asked, with his usual boyish directness—

"Has anything happened? Have I done anything wrong?"

"No, no," returned Don Juan hurriedly. "But, you see, it's time that you should think of your future—or at least prepare for it. I mean you ought to have some more regular education. You will have to go to school. It's too bad," he added fretfully, with a certain impatient forgetfulness of Clarence's presence, and as if following his own thought. "Just as you are becoming of service to me, and justifying your ridiculous position here—and all this d—d nonsense that's gone before—I mean, of course, Clarence," he interrupted himself, catching sight of the boy's whitening cheek and darkening eye, "I mean, you know—this ridiculousness of my keeping you from school at your age, and trying to teach you myself don't you see.:

"You think it is—ridiculous," repeated Clarence, with dogged persistency.

"I mean *I* am ridiculous," said Don Juan hastily. "There! there! let's say no more about it. To-morrow we'll ride over to San José and see the Father Secretary at the Jesuits' College about your entering at once. It's a good school, and you'll always be near the rancho!" And so the interview ended.

I am afraid that Clarence's first idea was to run away. There are few experiences more crushing to an ingenuous nature than the sudden revelation of the aspect in which it is regarded by others. The unfortunate Clarence, conscious only of his loyalty to his cousin's interest and what he believed were the duties of his position, awoke to find that position "ridiculous." In an afternoon's gloomy ride through the lonely hills, and later m the sleepless solitude of his room at night, he concluded that his cousin was right. He would go to school; he would study hard—so hard that in a little, a very little while, he could make a living for himself. He awoke contented. It was the blessing of youth, that this resolve and execution seemed as one and the same thing.

The next day found him installed as a pupil and boarder in the college. Don

Juan's position and Spanish predilections naturally made his relation acceptable to the faculty; but Clarence could not help perceiving that Father Sobriente, the Principal, regarded him at times with a thoughtful curiosity that made him suspect that his cousin had especially bespoken that attention, and that he occasionally questioned him on his antecedents in a way that made him dread a renewal of the old questioning about his progenitor. For the rest, he was a polished, cultivated man; yet, in the characteristic, material criticism of youth, I am afraid that Clarence chiefly identified him as a priest with large hands, whose soft palms seemed to be cushioned with kindness, and whose equally large feet, encased in extraordinary shapeless shoes of undyed leather, seemed to tread down noiselessly—rather than to ostentatiously crush—the obstacles that beset the path of the young student. In the cloistered galleries of the court-yard Clarence sometimes felt himself borne down by the protecting weight of this paternal hand; in the midnight silence of the dormitory he fancied he was often conscious of the soft browsing tread and snuffly muffled breathing of his elephantine-footed mentor.

His relations with his school-fellows were at first far from pleasant. Whether they suspected favoritism; whether they resented that old and unsympathetic manner which sprang from his habits of association with his elders; or whether they rested their objections on the broader grounds of his being a stranger, I do not know, but they presently passed from cruel sneers to physical opposition. It was then found that this gentle and reserved youth had retained certain objectionable, rude, direct, rustic qualities of fist and foot, and that, violating all rules and disdaining the pomp and circumstance of school-boy warfare, of which he knew nothing, he simply thrashed a few of his equals out of hand, with or without ceremony, as the occasion or the insult happened. In this emergency one of the seniors was selected to teach, this youthful savage his proper position. A challenge was given, and accepted by Clarence with a feverish alacrity that surprised himself as much as his adversary. This was a youth of eighteen, his superior in size and skill. The first blow bathed Clarence's face in his own blood. But the sanguinary chrism, to the alarm of the spectators, effected an instantaneous and unhallowed change in the boy. Instantly closing with his adversary, he sprang at his throat like an animal, and locking his arm around his neck began to strangle him. Blind to the blows that rained upon him, he eventually bore his staggering enemy by sheer onset and surprise to the earth. Amidst the general alarm, the strength of half a dozen hastily summoned teachers was necessary to unlock his hold. Even then he struggled to renew the conflict. But his adversary had disappeared, and from that day forward Clarence was never again molested.

Seated before Father Sobriente in the infirmary, with swollen and bandaged face, and eyes that still seemed to see everything m the murky light of his own blood, Clarence felt the soft weight of the father's hand upon his knee.

"My son," said the priest gently, "you are not of our religion, or I should claim as a right to ask a question of your own heart at this moment. But as to a good friend, Claro, a good, friend," he continued, patting the boy's knee, "you will tell me, old Father Sobrente, frankly and truthfully, as is your habit, one little thing. Were you not afraid?"

"No," said Clarence doggedly. "I'll lick him again to-morrow."

"Softly, my son! It was not of *him* I speak, but of something more terrible and awful. Were you not afraid of—of"—he paused, and suddenly darting his clear eyes into the very depths of Clarence's soul, added—"of *yourself?*"

The boy started, shuddered, and burst into tears.

"So, so", said the priest gently, "we have found our real enemy. Good! Now, by the grace of God, my little warrior, we shall fight *him* and conquer."

Whether Clarence profited by this lesson, or whether this brief exhibition of his quality prevented, any repetition of the cause, the episode was soon forgotten. As his school-fellows had never been his associates or confidants, it mattered little to him whether they feared or respected him, or were hypocritically obsequious, after the fashion of the weaker. His studies, at all events, profited by this lack of distraction. Already his two years of desultory and omnivorous reading had given him a facile familiarity with many things, which left him utterly free of the timidity, awkwardness, or non-interest of a beginner. His usually reserved manner, which, had been lack of expression rather than of conviction, had deceived, his tutors. The audacity of a mind that had never been dominated by others, and owed no allegiance to precedent, made his merely superficial progress something marvelous.

At the end of the first year he was a phenomenal scholar, who seemed capable of anything. Nevertheless, Father Sobriente had an interview with Don Juan, and as a result Clarence was slightly kept back in his studies, a little more freedom from the rules was conceded to him, and he was even encouraged to take some diversion. Of such was the privilege to visit the neighboring town of Santa Clara unrestricted and unattended. He had always been liberally furnished with pocket-money, for which, in his companionless state and Spartan habits, he had a singular and unboyish contempt. Nevertheless, he always appeared dressed with scrupulous neatness, and was rather distinguished-looking in his older reserve and melancholy self-reliance.

Lounging one afternoon along the Alameda, a leafy avenue set out by the early Mission Fathers between the village of San José and the convent of Santa Clara, he saw a double file of young girls from the convent approaching, on their usual promenade. A view of this procession being the fondest ambition of the San José collegian, and especially interdicted and circumvented by the good Fathers attending the college excursions, Clarence felt for it the profound indifference of a boy who, in the intermediate temperate zone of fifteen years, thinks that he is no longer young and romantic! He was passing them with a careless glance, when a pair of deep violet eyes caught his own under the broad shade of a coquettishly beribboned hat, even as it had once looked at him from the depths of a calico sun-bonnet. Susy! He started, and would have spoken; but with a quick little gesture of caution and a meaning glance at the two nuns who walked at the head and foot of the file, she indicated him to follow. He did so at a respectful distance, albeit wondering. A little further on Susy dropped her handkerchief, and was obliged to dart out and run back to the end of the file to recover it. But she gave another swift glance of her blue eyes as she snatched it up and demurely ran back to her place. The procession passed on, but when Clarence reached the spot where she had paused he saw a three-cornered bit of paper lying in the grass. He was too discreet to pick it up while the girls were still in sight, but continued on, returning to it later. It contained a few words in a school-girl's hand, hastily scrawled in pencil: "Come to the south wall near the big pear-tree at six."

Delighted as Clarence felt, he was at the same time embarrassed. He could not understand the necessity of this mysterious rendezvous. He knew that if she was a scholar she was under certain conventual restraints; but with the privileges of his position and friendship with his teachers, he believed that Father Sobriente would easily procure him an interview with this old playfellow, of whom he had often spoken, and who was, with himself, the sole survivor of his tragical past. And trusted as he was by Sobriente, there was something in this clandestine though innocent rendezvous that went against his loyalty. Nevertheless, he kept the appointment, and at the stated time was at the south wall of the convent, over which the gnarled boughs of the distinguishing pear-tree hung. Hard by in the wall was a grated wicket door that seemed unused.

Would she appear among the boughs or on the edge of the wall? Either would be like the old Susy. But to his surprise he heard the sound of the key turning in the lock. The grated door suddenly swung on its hinges, and Susy slipped out. Grasping his hand, she said, "Let's run, Clarence," and before he could reply she started off with him at a rapid pace. Down the lane they flew—very much, as it seemed to Clarence's fancy, as they had flown from the old emigrant wagon on the prairie, four years before. He glanced at the fluttering, fairylike figure beside him. She had grown taller and more graceful; she was dressed in exquisite taste, with a minuteness of luxurious detail that bespoke the spoilt child; but there was the same prodigal outburst of rippling, golden hair down her back and shoulders, violet eyes, capricious little mouth, and the same delicate hands and feet he had remembered. He would have preferred a more deliberate survey, but with a shake of her head and an hysteric little laugh she only said, "Run, Clarence, run," and again darted forward. Arriving at the cross-street, they turned, the corner, and halted breathlessly.

"But you're not running away from school, Susy, are you?" said Clarence anxiously.

"Only a little bit. Just enough to get ahead of the other girls," she said, rearranging her brown curls and tilted hat. "You see, Clarence," she condescended to explain, with a sudden assumption of older superiority, "mother's here at the hotel all this week, and I'm allowed to go home every night, like a day scholar. Only there's three or four other girls that go out at the same time with me, and one of the Sisters, and to-day I got ahead of 'em just to see *you.*"

"But"—began Clarence.

"Oh, it's all right; the other girls knew it, and helped me. They don't start out for half an hour yet, and they'll say I've just run ahead, and when they and the Sister get to the hotel I'll be there already—don't you see?"

"Yes," said Clarence dubiously.

"And we'll go to an ice-cream saloon now, sha'n't we? There's a nice one near the hotel. I've got some money," she added quickly, as Clarence looked embarrassed.

"So have I," said Clarence, with a faint accession of color. "Let's go!" She had relinquished his hand to smooth out her frock, and they were walking side by side at a more moderate pace. "But," he continued, clinging to his first idea with masculine persistence, and anxious to assure his companion of his power, of his position, "I'm in the college, and Father Sobriente, who knows your lady superior, is a good friend of mine and gives me privileges; and—and—when he knows that you and I used to play together—why, he'll fix it that we may see each other whenever we want."

"Oh you silly!" said Susy. "*What!*—when you're"—

"When I'm *what*?"

The young girl shot a violet blue ray from under her broad hat. "Why—when we're grown up now?" Then with a certain precision, "Why, they're *very* particular about young gentlemen! Why, Clarence, if they suspected that you and I were"—Another violet ray from under the hat completed this unfinished sentence.

Pleased and yet confused, Clarence looked straight ahead with deepening color. "Why," continued Susy, "Mary Rogers, that was walking with me, thought you were ever so old—and a distinguished Spaniard! And I," she said abruptly—"haven't I grown? Tell me, Clarence," with her old appealing impatience, "have't I grown? Do tell me!"

"Very much," said Clarence.

"And isn't this frock pretty—it's only my second best—but I've a prettier one with lace all down in front; but isn't this one pretty, Clarence, tell me?"

Clarence thought the frock and its fair owner perfection, and said so. Whereat Susy, as if suddenly aware of the presence of passers-by, assumed an air of severe propriety, dropped her hands by her side, and with an affected conscientiousness walked on, a little further from Clarence's side, until they reached the ice-cream saloon.

"Get a table near the back, Clarence," she said, in a confidential whisper, "where they can't see us—and strawberry, you know, for the lemon and vanilla here are just horrid!"

They took their seats a Kind of rustic arbor in the rear of the shop, which gave them the appearance of two youthful but somewhat over-dressed and over-conscious shepherds. There was an interval of slight awkwardness, which Susy endeavored to displace. "There has been," she remarked, with easy conversational lightness, "quite an excitement about our French teacher being changed. The girls in our class think it most disgraceful."

And this was all she could say after a separation of four years! Clarence was desperate, but as yet idealess and voiceless. At last, with an effort over his spoon, he gasped a floating recollection: "Do you still like flapjacks, Susy?"

"Oh, yes," with a laugh, "but we don't have them now."

"And Mose" (a black pointer, who used to yelp when Susy sang), "does he still sing with you?"

"Oh, *he's* been lost ever so long," said Susy composedly; "but I've got a Newfoundland and a spaniel and a black pony;" and here, with a rapid inventory of her other personal effects, she drifted into some desultory details of the devotion of her adopted parents, whom she now readily spoke of as "papa" and "mamma," with evidently no disturbing recollection of the dead. From which it appeared that the Peytons were very rich, and, in addition to their possessions in the lower country, owned a ranche in Santa Clara and a house in San Francisco. Like all children, her strongest impressions were the most recent. In the vain hope to lead her back to this material yesterday, he said—

"You remember Jim Hooker?"

"Oh, *he* ran away, when you left. But just think of it! The other day, when papa and I went into a big restaurant in San Francisco, who should be there *waiting* on the table—yes, Clarence, a real waiter—but Jim Hooker! Papa spoke to him; but of course," with a slight elevation of her pretty chin, "*I* couldn't, you know; fancy—a waiter!"

The story of how Jim Hooker had personated him stopped short upon Clarence's lips. He could not bring himself now to add that revelation to the contempt of his small companion, which, in spite of its na?veté somewhat grated on his sensibilities.

"Clarence," she said, suddenly turning towards him mysteriously, and indicating the shopman and his assistants, "I really believe these people suspect us."

"Of what?" said the practical Clarence.

"Don't be silly! Don't you see how they are staring?"

Clarence was really unable to detect the least curiosity on the part of the shop-man, or that any one exhibited the slightest concern in him or his companion. But he felt a return of the embarrassed pleasure he was conscious of a moment before. "Then you're living with your father?" said Susy, changing the subject.

"You mean my cousin," said Clarence, smiling. "You know my father died long before I ever knew you."

"Yes; that's what you used to say, Clarence, but papa says it isn't so." But see-ing the boy's wondering eyes fixed on her with a troubled expression, she added quickly, "Oh, then, he is your cousin!"

"Well, I think I ought to know," said Clarence, with a smile, that was, however, far from comfortable, and a quick return of his old unpleasant recollections of the Peytons. "Why, I was brought to him by one of his friends." And Clarence gave a rapid boyish summary of his journey from Sacramento, and Flynn's discovery of the letter addressed to Silsbee. But before he had concluded he was conscious that Susy was by no means interested in these details, nor in the least affected by the pass-ing allusion to her dead father and his relation to Clarence's misadventures. With her rounded chin in her hand, she was slowly examining his face, with a certain mischievous yet demure abstraction. "I tell you what, Clarence," she said, when he had finished, "you ought to make your cousin get you one of those sombreros, and a nice gold-braided serape. They'd just suit you. And then—then you could ride up and down the Alameda when we are going by."

"But I'm coming to see you at—at your house, and at the convent," he said ea-gerly. "Father Sobriente and my cousin will fix it all right."

But Susy shook her head, with superior wisdom. "No; they must never know our secret!—neither papa nor mamma, especially mamma. And they mustn't know that we've met again—*after these years!*" It is impossible to describe the deep sig-nificance which Susy's blue eyes gave to this expression. After a pause she went on—

"No! We must never meet again, Clarence, unless Mary Rogers helps. She is my best, my *onliest* friend, and older than I; having had trouble herself, and being expressly forbidden to see him again. You can speak to her about Suzette—that's my name now; I was rechristened Suzette Alexandra Peyton by mamma. And now, Clarence," dropping her voice and glancing shyly around the saloon, "you may kiss me just once under my hat, for good-by." She adroitly slanted her broad - brimmed hat towards the front of the shop, and in its shadow advanced her fresh young cheek to Clarence.

Coloring and laughing, the boy pressed his lips to it twice. Then Susy arose, with the faintest affectation of a sigh, shook out her skirt, drew on her gloves with the greatest gravity, and saying, "Don't follow me further than the door—they're coming now," walked with supercilious dignity past the preoccupied proprietor and waiters to the entrance. Here she said, with marked civility, "Good-afternoon, Mr. Brant," and tripped away towards the hotel. Clarence lingered for a moment to look after the lithe and elegant little figure, with its shining undulations of hair that fell over the back and shoulders of her white frock like a golden mantle, and then turned away in the opposite direction.

He walked home in a state, as it seemed to him, of absurd perplexity. There were many reasons why his encounter with Susy should have been of unmixed pleasure. She had remembered him of her own free will, and, in spite of the change in her fortune, had made the first advances. Her doubts about her future interviews had affected him but little; still less, I fear, did he think of the other changes in her character and disposition, for he was of that age when they added only a piquancy and fascination to her—as of one who, in spite of her weakness of nature, was still devoted to him! But he was painfully conscious that this meeting had revived in him all the fears, vague uneasiness, and sense of wrong that had haunted his first boyhood, and which he thought he had buried at El Refugio four years ago. Susy's allusion to his father and the reiteration of Peyton's skepticism awoke in his older intellect the first feeling of suspicion that was compatible with his open nature. Was this recurring reticence and mystery due to any act of his father's? But, looking back upon it in after-years, he concluded that the incident of that day was a premonition rather than a recollection.

CHAPTER XI.

WHEN he reached the college the Angelus had long since rung. In the corridor he met one of the Fathers, who, instead of questioning him, returned his salutation with a grave gentleness that struck him. He had turned into Father Sobriente's quiet study with the intention of reporting himself, when he was disturbed, to find him in consultation with three or four of the faculty, who seemed to be thrown into some slight confusion by his entrance. Clarence was about to retire hurriedly when Father Sobriente, breaking up the council with a significant glance at the others, called him back. Confused and embarrassed, with a dread of something impending, the boy tried to avert it by a hurried account of his meeting with Susy, and his hopes of Father Sobriente's counsel and assistance. Taking upon himself the idea of suggesting Susy's escapade, he confessed the fault. The old man gazed into his frank smile. "I was just thinking of giving you a holiday with—with Don Juan Robinson." The unusual substitution of this final title for the habitual "your cousin" struck Clarence uneasily. "But we will speak of that later. Sit down, my son; I am not busy. We shall talk a little. Father Pedro says you are getting on fluently with your translations. That is excellent, my son, excellent."

Clarence's face beamed with relief and pleasure. His vague fears began to dissipate.

"And you translate even from, dictation! Good! We have an hour to spare, and you shall give to me a specimen of your skill. Eh? Good! I will walk here and dictate to you in my poor English, and you shall sit here and render it to me in your good Spanish. Eh? So we shall amuse and instruct ourselves."

Clarence smiled. These sporadic moments of instruction and admonition were not unusual to the good Father. He cheerfully seated himself at the Padre's table before a blank sheet of paper, with a pen in his hand. Father Sobriente paced the apartment, with his usual heavy but noiseless tread. To his surprise, the good priest, after an exhaustive pinch of snuff, blew his nose, and began, in his most lugubrious style of pulpit exhortation:—

"It has been written that the sins of the father shall be visited upon the children, and the unthinking and worldly have sought refuge from this law by declaring it harsh and cruel. Miserable and blind! For do we not see that the wicked man, who in the pride of his power and vainglory is willing to risk punishment to *himself*—and believes it to be courage—must pause before the awful mandate that condemns an equal suffering to those he loves, which he cannot withhold or suffer for? In the spectacle of these innocents struggling against disgrace, perhaps disease, poverty, or desertion, what avails his haughty, all-defying spirit? Let us imagine, Clarence.”

“Sir?” said the literal Clarence, pausing in his exercise.

“I mean,” continued the priest, with a slight cough, “let the thoughtful man picture a father: a desperate, self-willed man, who scorned the laws of God and society—keeping only faith with a miserable subterfuge he called ‘honor,’ and re-lying only on his own courage and his knowledge of human weakness. Imagine him cruel and bloody—a gambler by profession, an out-law among men, an outcast from the Church; voluntarily abandoning friends and family,—the wife he should have cherished, the son he should have reared and educated—for the gratification of his deadly passions. Yet imagine that man suddenly confronted with the thought of that heritage of shame and disgust which he had brought upon his innocent offspring—to whom he cannot give even his own desperate recklessness to sustain its vicarious suffering. What must be the feelings of a parent”—

“Father Sobriente,” said Clarence softly.

To the boy’s surprise, scarcely had he spoken when the soft protecting palm of the priest was already upon his shoulder, and the snuffy but kindly upper lip, trembling with some strange emotion, close beside his cheek.

“What is it, Clarence?” he said hurriedly. “Speak, my son, without fear! You would ask”—

“I only wanted to know if ‘padre’ takes a masculine verb here,” replied Clarence naively.

Father Sobriente blew his nose violently.

“Truly—though used for either gender, by the context masculine,” he responded gravely. “Ah,” he added, leaning over Clarence, and scanning his work hastily, “Good, very good! And now, possibly,” he continued, passing his hand like a damp sponge over his heated brow, “we shall reverse our exercise. I shall deliver to you in Spanish what you shall render back in English, eh? And—let us consider—we shall make something more familiar and narrative, eh?”

To this Clarence, somewhat bored by these present solemn abstractions, assented gladly, and took up his pen. Father Sobriente, resuming his noiseless pacing, began:

“On the fertile plains of Guadalajara lived a certain caballero, possessed of flocks and lands, and a wife and son. But, being also possessed of a fiery and roving nature, he did not value them as he did perilous adventure, feats of arms, and sanguinary encounters. To this may be added riotous excesses, gambling and drunkenness, which in time decreased his patrimony, even as his rebellious and quarrelsome spirit had alienated his family and neighbors. His wife, borne down by shame and sorrow, died while her son was still an infant. In a fit of equal remorse and recklessness the caballero married again within the year. But the new wife was of a temper and bearing as bitter as her consort. Violent quarrels ensued between them, ending in the husband abandoning his wife and son, and leaving St. Louis—I should say Guadalajara—for, ever. Joining some adventurers in a foreign land, under an assumed name, he pursued his reckless course, until, by one or two acts of outlawry, he made his return to civilization impossible. The deserted wife and step-mother of his child coldly accepted the situation, forbidding his name to be spoken again in her presence, announced that he was dead, and kept the knowledge of his existence from his own son, whom she placed under the charge of her sister. But the sister managed to secretly communicate with the outlawed father, and, under a pretext, arranged between them, of sending the boy to another relation, actually dispatched the innocent child to his unworthy parent. Perhaps stirred by remorse, the infamous man"—

"Stop!" said Clarence suddenly.

He had thrown down his pen, and was standing erect and rigid before the Father.

"You are trying to tell me something, Father Sobriente," he said, with an effort. "Speak out, I implore you. I can stand anything but this mystery. I am no longer a child. I have a right to know all. This that you are telling me is no fable—I see it in your face, Father Sobriente; it is the story of—of"—

"Your father, Clarence," said the priest, in a trembling voice.

The boy drew back, with a white face. "My father!" he repeated. "Living, or dead?"

"Living, when you first left your home," said the old man hurriedly, seizing Clarence's hand, "for it was he who in the name of your cousin sent for you. Living—yes, while you were here, for it was he who for the past three years stood in the shadow of this assumed cousin, Don Juan, and at last sent you to this school. Living, Clarence, yes; but living under a name and reputation that would have blasted you! And now ***dead***—dead in Mexico, shot as an insurgent and in a still desperate career! May God have mercy on his soul!"

"Dead!" repeated Clarence, trembling, "only now?"

"The news of the insurrection and his fate came only an hour since," continued the Padre quickly; "his complicity with it and his identity were known only to Don Juan. He would have spared you any knowledge of the truth, even as this dead man would; but I and my brothers thought otherwise. I have broken it to you badly, my son, but forgive me?"

An hysterical laugh broke from Clarence, and the priest recoiled, before him. "Forgive ***you!*** What was this man to me?" he said, with boyish vehemence. "He never ***loved*** me! He deserted me; he made my life a lie. He never sought me, came near me, or stretched a hand to me that I could take?"

"Hush! hush!" said the priest, with a horrified look, laying his huge hand upon the boy's shoulder and bearing him down to his seat. "You know not what you say. Think—think, Clarence! Was there none of all those who have befriended you— who were kind to you in your wanderings—to whom your heart turned unconsciously? Think, Clarence! You yourself have spoken to me of such a one. Let your heart speak again, for his sake—for the sake of the dead."

A gentler light suffused the boy's eyes, and he started. Catching convulsively at his companion's sleeve, he said in an eager, boyish whisper, "There was one, a wicked, desperate man, whom they all feared—Flynn, who brought me from the mines. Yes, I thought that he was my cousin's loyal friend—more than all the rest; and I told him everything—all, that I never told the man I thought my cousin, or any one, or even you; and I think, I think, Father, I liked him best of all. I thought since it was wrong," he continued, with a trembling smile, "for I was foolishly fond even of the way the others feared him, he that I feared not, and who was so kind to me. Yet he, too, left me without a word, and when I would have followed him"— But the boy broke down, and buried, his face in his hands.

"No, no, said Father Sobriente, with eager persistence, "that was his foolish pride to spare you the knowledge of your kinship with one so feared, and part of the blind and mistaken penance he had laid upon himself. For even at that moment of your boyish indignation, he never was so fond of you as then. Yes, my poor boy, this man, to whom God led your wandering feet at Deadman's Gulch; the man who brought you here, and by some secret hold—I know not what—on Don Juan's past, persuaded him to assume to be your relation; this man Flynn, this Jackson Brant the gambler, this Hamilton Brant the gambler, this Hamilton Brant the outlaw—*was your father!* Ah, yes! Weep on, my son; each tear of love and forgiveness from thee hath vicarious power to wash away his sin."

With a single sweep of his protecting hand he drew Clarence towards his breast, until the boy slowly sank upon his knees at his feet. Then, lifting his eyes towards the ceiling, he said softly in an older tongue, "And *thou*, too, unhappy and perturbed spirit, rest!"

It was nearly dawn when the good Padre wiped the last tears from Clarence's clearer eyes. "And now, my son," he said, with a gentle smile, as he rose to his feet, "let us not forget the living. Although your step mother has, through her own act, no legal claim upon you, far be it from me to indicate your attitude towards her. Enough that *you* are independent." He turned, and, opening a drawer in his secretaire, took out a bank-book, and placed it in the hands of the wondering boy.

"It was *his* wish, Clarence, that even after his death you should never have to prove your kinship to claim your rights. Taking advantage of the boyish deposit you had left with Mr. Carden at the bank, with his connivance and in your name he added to it, month by month and year by year; Mr. Carden cheerfully accepting the trust and management of the fund. The seed thus sown has produced a thousandfold, Clarence, beyond all expectations. You are not only free, my son, but of yourself and in whatever name you choose—your own master."

"I shall keep my father's name," said the boy simply.

"Amen!" said Father Sobriente.

Here closes the chronicle of Clarence Brant's boyhood. How he sustained his name and independence in after-years, and who, of those already mentioned in these pages, helped him to make or mar it, may be a matter for future record.

The Codes Of Hammurabi And Moses
W. W. Davies

QTY

The discovery of the Hammurabi Code is one of the greatest achievements of archaeology, and is of paramount interest, not only to the student of the Bible, but also to all those interested in ancient history...

Religion   ISBN: *1-59462-338-4*   **Pages:132**
MSRP *$12.95*

The Theory of Moral Sentiments
Adam Smith

QTY

This work from 1749. contains original theories of conscience amd moral judgment and it is the foundation for systemof morals.

Philosophy ISBN: *1-59462-777-0*   **Pages:536**
MSRP *$19.95*

Jessica's First Prayer
Hesba Stretton

QTY

In a screened and secluded corner of one of the many railway-bridges which span the streets of London there could be seen a few years ago, from five o'clock every morning until half past eight, a tidily set-out coffee-stall, consisting of a trestle and board, upon which stood two large tin cans, with a small fire of charcoal burning under each so as to keep the coffee boiling during the early hours of the morning when the work-people were thronging into the city on their way to their daily toil...

Childrens   ISBN: *1-59462-373-2*   **Pages:84**
MSRP *$9.95*

My Life and Work
Henry Ford

QTY

Henry Ford revolutionized the world with his implementation of mass production for the Model T automobile. Gain valuable business insight into his life and work with his own auto-biography... "We have only started on our development of our country we have not as yet, with all our talk of wonderful progress, done more than scratch the surface. The progress has been wonderful enough but..."

Biographies/   ISBN: *1-59462-198-5*   **Pages:300**
MSRP *$21.95*

The Art of Cross-Examination
Francis Wellman

QTY

I presume it is the experience of every author, after his first book is published upon an important subject, to be almost overwhelmed with a wealth of ideas and illustrations which could readily have been included in his book, and which to his own mind, at least, seem to make a second edition inevitable. Such certainly was the case with me; and when the first edition had reached its sixth impression in five months, I rejoiced to learn that it seemed to my publishers that the book had met with a sufficiently favorable reception to justify a second and considerably enlarged edition. ...

Pages:412

Reference ISBN: *1-59462-647-2*   *MSRP $19.95*

On the Duty of Civil Disobedience
Henry David Thoreau

QTY

Thoreau wrote his famous essay, On the Duty of Civil Disobedience, as a protest against an unjust but popular war and the immoral but popular institution of slave-owning. He did more than write—he declined to pay his taxes, and was hauled off to gaol in consequence. Who can say how much this refusal of his hastened the end of the war and of slavery ?

Law ISBN: *1-59462-747-9*   **Pages:48**
MSRP $7.45

Dream Psychology Psychoanalysis for Beginners
Sigmund Freud

QTY

Sigmund Freud, born Sigismund Schlomo Freud (May 6, 1856 - September 23, 1939), was a Jewish-Austrian neurologist and psychiatrist who co-founded the psychoanalytic school of psychology. Freud is best known for his theories of the unconscious mind, especially involving the mechanism of repression; his redefinition of sexual desire as mobile and directed towards a wide variety of objects; and his therapeutic techniques, especially his understanding of transference in the therapeutic relationship and the presumed value of dreams as sources of insight into unconscious desires.

Pages:196

Psychology ISBN: *1-59462-905-6*   *MSRP $15.45*

The Miracle of Right Thought
Orison Swett Marden

QTY

Believe with all of your heart that you will do what you were made to do. When the mind has once formed the habit of holding cheerful, happy, prosperous pictures, it will not be easy to form the opposite habit. It does not matter how improbable or how far away this realization may see, or how dark the prospects may be, if we visualize them as best we can, as vividly as possible, hold tenaciously to them and vigorously struggle to attain them, they will gradually become actualized, realized in the life. But a desire, a longing without endeavor, a yearning abandoned or held indifferently will vanish without realization.

Pages:360

Self Help ISBN: *1-59462-644-8*   *MSRP $25.45*

QTY

☐ **The Rosicrucian Cosmo-Conception Mystic Christianity** by *Max Heindel* ISBN: *1-59462-188-8* **$38.95**
The Rosicrucian Cosmo-conception is not dogmatic, neither does it appeal to any other authority than the reason of the student. It is: not controversial, but is: sent forth in the, hope that it may help to clear...
New Age/Religion Pages 646

☐ **Abandonment To Divine Providence** by *Jean-Pierre de Caussade* ISBN: *1-59462-228-0* **$25.95**
"The Rev. Jean Pierre de Caussade was one of the most remarkable spiritual writers of the Society of Jesus in France in the 18th Century. His death took place at Toulouse in 1751. His works have gone through many editions and have been republished...
Inspirational/Religion Pages 400

☐ **Mental Chemistry** by *Charles Haanel* ISBN: *1-59462-192-6* **$23.95**
Mental Chemistry allows the change of material conditions by combining and appropriately utilizing the power of the mind. Much like applied chemistry creates something new and unique out of careful combinations of chemicals the mastery of mental chemistry...
New Age Pages 354

☐ **The Letters of Robert Browning and Elizabeth Barret Barrett 1845-1846 vol II** ISBN: *1-59462-193-4* **$35.95**
by *Robert Browning* and *Elizabeth Barrett*
Biographies Pages 596

☐ **Gleanings In Genesis (volume I)** by *Arthur W. Pink* ISBN: *1-59462-130-6* **$27.45**
Appropriately has Genesis been termed "the seed plot of the Bible" for in it we have, in germ form, almost all of the great doctrines which are afterwards fully developed in the books of Scripture which follow...
Religion/Inspirational Pages 420

☐ **The Master Key** by *L. W. de Laurence* ISBN: *1-59462-001-6* **$30.95**
In no branch of human knowledge has there been a more lively increase of the spirit of research during the past few years than in the study of Psychology, Concentration and Mental Discipline. The requests for authentic lessons in Thought Control, Mental Discipline and...
New Age/Business Pages 422

☐ **The Lesser Key Of Solomon Goetia** by *L. W. de Laurence* ISBN: *1-59462-092-X* **$9.95**
This translation of the first book of the "Lemegton" which is now for the first time made accessible to students of Talismanic Magic was done, after careful collation and edition, from numerous Ancient Manuscripts in Hebrew, Latin, and French...
New Age/Occult Pages 92

☐ **Rubaiyat Of Omar Khayyam** by *Edward Fitzgerald* ISBN: *1-59462-332-5* **$13.95**
Edward Fitzgerald, whom the world has already learned, in spite of his own efforts to remain within the shadow of anonymity, to look upon as one of the rarest poets of the century, was born at Bredfield, in Suffolk, on the 31st of March, 1809. He was the third son of John Purcell...
Music Pages 172

☐ **Ancient Law** by *Henry Maine* ISBN: *1-59462-128-4* **$29.95**
The chief object of the following pages is to indicate some of the earliest ideas of mankind, as they are reflected in Ancient Law, and to point out the relation of those ideas to modern thought.
Religiom/History Pages 452

☐ **Far-Away Stories** by *William J. Locke* ISBN: *1-59462-129-2* **$19.45**
"Good wine needs no bush, but a collection of mixed vintages does. And this book is just such a collection. Some of the stories I do not want to remain buried for ever in the museum files of dead magazine-numbers an author's not unpardonable vanity..."
Fiction Pages 272

☐ **Life of David Crockett** by *David Crockett* ISBN: *1-59462-250-7* **$27.45**
"Colonel David Crockett was one of the most remarkable men of the times in which he lived. Born in humble life, but gifted with a strong will, an indomitable courage, and unremitting perseverance...
Biographies/New Age Pages 424

☐ **Lip-Reading** by *Edward Nitchie* ISBN: *1-59462-206-X* **$25.95**
Edward B. Nitchie, founder of the New York School for the Hard of Hearing, now the Nitchie School of Lip-Reading, Inc, wrote "LIP-READING Principles and Practice". The development and perfecting of this meritorious work on lip-reading was an undertaking...
How-to Pages 400

☐ **A Handbook of Suggestive Therapeutics, Applied Hypnotism, Psychic Science** ISBN: *1-59462-214-0* **$24.95**
by *Henry Munro*
Health/New Age/Health/Self-help Pages 376

☐ **A Doll's House: and Two Other Plays** by *Henrik Ibsen* ISBN: *1-59462-112-8* **$19.95**
Henrik Ibsen created this classic when in revolutionary 1848 Rome. Introducing some striking concepts in playwriting for the realist genre, this play has been studied the world over.
Fiction/Classics/Plays 308

☐ **The Light of Asia** by *sir Edwin Arnold* ISBN: *1-59462-204-3* **$13.95**
In this poetic masterpiece, Edwin Arnold describes the life and teachings of Buddha. The man who was to become known as Buddha to the world was born as Prince Gautama of India but he rejected the worldly riches and abandoned the reigns of power when...
Religion/History/Biographies Pages 170

☐ **The Complete Works of Guy de Maupassant** by *Guy de Maupassant* ISBN: *1-59462-157-8* **$16.95**
"For days and days, nights and nights, I had dreamed of that first kiss which was to consecrate our engagement, and I knew not on what spot I should put my lips..."
Fiction/Classics Pages 240

☐ **The Art of Cross-Examination** by *Francis L. Wellman* ISBN: *1-59462-309-0* **$26.95**
Written by a renowned trial lawyer, Wellman imparts his experience and uses case studies to explain how to use psychology to extract desired information through questioning.
How-to/Science/Reference Pages 408

☐ **Answered or Unanswered?** by *Louisa Vaughan* ISBN: *1-59462-248-5* **$10.95**
Miracles of Faith in China
Religion Pages 112

☐ **The Edinburgh Lectures on Mental Science (1909)** by *Thomas* ISBN: *1-59462-008-3* **$11.95**
This book contains the substance of a course of lectures recently given by the writer in the Queen Street Hail, Edinburgh. Its purpose is to indicate the Natural Principles governing the relation between Mental Action and Material Conditions...
New Age/Psychology Pages 148

☐ **Ayesha** by *H. Rider Haggard* ISBN: *1-59462-301-5* **$24.95**
Verily and indeed it is the unexpected that happens! Probably if there was one person upon the earth from whom the Editor of this, and of a certain previous history, did not expect to hear again...
Classics Pages 380

☐ **Ayala's Angel** by *Anthony Trollope* ISBN: *1-59462-352-X* **$29.95**
The two girls were both pretty, but Lucy who was twenty-one who supposed to be simple and comparatively unattractive, whereas Ayala was credited, as her Bombwhat romantic name might show, with poetic charm and a taste for romance. Ayala when her father died was nineteen...
Fiction Pages 484

☐ **The American Commonwealth** by *James Bryce* ISBN: *1-59462-286-8* **$34.45**
An interpretation of American democratic political theory. It examines political mechanics and society from the perspective of Scotsman James Bryce
Politics Pages 572

☐ **Stories of the Pilgrims** by *Margaret P. Pumphrey* ISBN: *1-59462-116-0* **$17.95**
This book explores pilgrims religious oppression in England as well as their escape to Holland and eventual crossing to America on the Mayflower, and their early days in New England...
History Pages 268

QTY

The Fasting Cure *by Sinclair Upton*   ISBN: *1-59462-222-1* **$13.95**
In the Cosmopolitan Magazine for May, 1910, and in the Contemporary Review (London) for April, 1910, I published an article dealing with my experi-
ences in fasting. I have written a great many magazine articles, but never one which attracted so much attention... New Age/Self Help/Health Pages 164

Hebrew Astrology *by Sepharial*   ISBN: *1-59462-308-2* **$13.45**
In these days of advanced thinking it is a matter of common observation that we have left many of the old landmarks behind and that we are now pressing
forward to greater heights and to a wider horizon than that which represented the mind-content of our progenitors...   Astrology Pages 144

Thought Vibration or The Law of Attraction in the Thought World ISBN: *1-59462-127-6* **$12.95**

by William Walker Atkinson   Psychology/Religion Pages 144

Optimism *by Helen Keller*   ISBN: *1-59462-108-X* **$15.95**
Helen Keller was blind, deaf, and mute since 19 months old, yet famously learned how to overcome these handicaps, communicate with the world, and
spread her lectures promoting optimism. An inspiring read for everyone...   Biographies/Inspirational Pages 84

Sara Crewe *by Frances Burnett*   ISBN: *1-59462-360-0*   **$9.45**
In the first place, Miss Minchin lived in London. Her home was a large, dull, tall one, in a large, dull square, where all the houses were alike, and all the
sparrows were alike, and where all the door-knockers made the same heavy sound...   Childrens/Classic Pages 88

The Autobiography of Benjamin Franklin *by Benjamin Franklin*   ISBN: *1-59462-135-7*   **$24.95**
The Autobiography of Benjamin Franklin has probably been more extensively read than any other American historical work, and no other book of its kind
has had such ups and downs of fortune. Franklin lived for many years in England, where he was agent...   Biographies/History Pages 332

Name	
Email	
Telephone	
Address	
City, State ZIP	

☐ **Credit Card**   ☐ **Check / Money Order**

Credit Card Number	
Expiration Date	
Signature	

Please Mail to: Book Jungle
PO Box 2226
Champaign, IL 61825
or Fax to: 630-214-0564

ORDERING INFORMATION

web: *www.bookjungle.com*
email: *sales@bookjungle.com*
fax: *630-214-0564*
mail: *Book Jungle PO Box 2226 Champaign, IL 61825*
or PayPal *to sales@bookjungle.com*

Please contact us for bulk discounts

DIRECT-ORDER TERMS

**20% Discount if You Order
Two or More Books**
Free Domestic Shipping!
Accepted: Master Card, Visa,
Discover, American Express

www.ingramcontent.com/pod-product-compliance
Lightning Source LLC
Chambersburg PA
CBHW082016170626

46817CB00009B/3109